I0822636

THE DREAM CHRONICLES

Book Two

iBooks
Habent Sua Fata Libelli

iBooks
Manhanset House
Dering Harbor, New York 11965

bricktower@aol.com • www.ibooksinc.com

Library of Congress Cataloging-in-Publication Data

Rotenberg, David.
The Dream Chronicles, Book Two
p. cm.

1. Fiction—Science Fiction—General. 2. Fiction—Science Fiction—Time Travel. 3. Fiction—Science Fiction—Adventure Fiction, I. Title.

Book One, ISBN: 978-1-59687-520-3, Hardcover
Book Two, ISBN: 978-1-59687-521-0, Hardcover

THE DREAM CHRONICLES

Book Two

DEDICATION:

FOR SUSAN, JOEY, MARY, BETH AND BEAN

ACKNOWLEDGMENTS

With my sincere thanks to my readers without whom there would really be no point in writing and Mr. Colby's fine work on publishing the novel.

Table of Contents

Onward

Part Three

Entry A—from the Diary of the Suicided Man

(No Date was recorded for this entry)

So it's probably time for me to come clean about dreaming.

That which I have facilitated but have never been part of.

Everything changed when our Star Ship disappeared and the now infamous scattercast was received throughout the galaxy:

Your ship has passed through the Gateway. Here your navigation systems are useless because beyond here lie dreams.

But for over 400 years, since the brief benign and only Alien contact, no human has had dreams. Back then:

For Fear of Nightmares, humanity abandoned Dreaming.

Humanity used to dream and from those dreams came art and science–and danger. You could not investigate the cosmos without making mankind feel small, if not totally insignificant. And when humans feel small they resort to violence to prove that they are big and important. Even the production of art brings on danger. Violence, jealousy, xenophobia and pure racial hatred are not condoned by many but in the privacy of the artist's heart he or she is accessing them, whether consciously or not, to be sure the art is of the totality of the human expe-

rience. There simply is no love unless it's smashed up against hate. It was no accident that Jesus faced temptation in the desert. If one is not tempted with evil then being good is not an achievement.

But what you ask has this to do with dreaming. It has every thing to do with dreaming. Dreaming is the willingness to jump into the abyss without a safety net. Free falling backward down a well on a moonless night. To what? To glory or great pain. Is there glory without the possibility of pain–I think not.

The progeny of Lah Ran Soni El, one of the last humans who was surgically gene manipulated to dream navigate, are several generations away from their famous or infamous (since he originated the command for all Dream Navigators to cease dreaming) ancestor. And the likelihood that any one of them would have the complete gene coding to dream navigate is unlikely. But perhaps together they can do it.

I'm still fresh from Miro's slave show and the blood of the last Dream Navigator I surgically gene manipulated into being–Elijah Jaspers, the ship's canary–is still wet on my fingers, sticky in my hair and its fresh thick scent is still up my nose.

If I ever loved anyone but Olya, I loved him–him as a boy.

Elijah could dream on command then navigate within his dream with incredible courage and accuracy. He was a great talent.

It seems that the Dreamers we had the pirate captain, Tzu Ma Long, kidnap have nowhere near his talent but, no doubt, he tried to teach them what he knew.

But what did they learn? How to discern the depths of a painting, how to spot a person with special gifts, how to recognize in a poem that there is glory beneath the words. But these are only baby steps toward dreaming. And even if they find their way to Dreams they still need to find the skill and the courage to navigate in their dreams.

Others are data mining to find dreaming. Looking at the products of our formerly great dream culture is like looking at a lion in a zoo. You see the lion. You recognize that it is a lion but you are not the lion and only a fool would claim that he even understood what a lion is. So when the data miners find a flimsie or a flat face left over from the dreaming age–unless they have the gift–they know no more about dreaming than the person at the zoo knows about being a lion.

Some of us who lived through the age of dreaming pine for the products of dreaming.

I don't.

I pine for the free fall of dreaming itself.

It was no mistake that the "dream factories" began to break down the walls between artists and civilians–those who are in the light and those that sit in the dark. It was the central idea behind the ludicrously named reality television. Those folks weren't actors accessing dreams, these were people who watched actors and learned how to imitate them–form without content. They produced a whole world of still born dreams–empty, dead on arrival.

But how reassuring it all was. Those actors–those artists–are no different than us–I can watch people just like me on the flat screen.

But that's profoundly a lie. An artist makes the leap, faces the danger of entering the chaos of dreams–those who just watch, do not.

Then there was VR–be in the place, see the danger but never be in danger. It was from this that the drug companies made the leap to empathetics. No more silly looking goggles:

JUST TAKE THE PILL AND FEEL THE THRILL.

Who could forget that bit of ad copy?

But I never wanted the pill–I wanted the thrill–but it was beyond me–always beyond me.

What follows is my story. Heed the clues and you can find me. Or don't bother and find yourself–because you're here too–in the dreamless silence, falling–trapped forever on this side of the Gateway.

Chapter 1

Danazir Yi Qal

As the final parliamentary session of the Terran year began Danazir Yi Qal, President of the United Dominion of Planets, let her mind drift back to a time when Jedidiah Witt, her head of security, was corporeally alive. Back before Cyrus III of S3 had him hunted down. Back before Jedidiah had insisted that they institute the plan that implanted Jed's being in her chest just above her heart.

Back to the day less than half a Terran year ago of the first S3 attempt to assassinate her.

Jedidiah had warned her that the attack was imminent.

That morning, when she entered the UDP Senate chamber, she could sense that something was different. The constituency was the same—two members from most of the Dominion's planets—but there was something heavy in the air, a wariness.

The session itself had gone without a hitch. A few simple ritual-like bills were put forward and sent to committee—everything was sent to committee these days now that S3 had control of so many of the senators.

A brief row broke out between two female members who had a history of bad mouthing each other. After one had finally ended an interminable monologue that had no particular point, the other had risen on a point of order and said, "Every time you open your mouth you subtract from the sum of human knowledge. Even Demosthenes was shorter winded."

Danazir found the first part of the remark surprisingly clever for a woman for whom she had little intellectual respect. And she had no idea what the second part meant, let alone who Demosthenes was.

Near the end of the session she was surprised to see Jedidiah standing deep in the shadows at the back of the gallery. He nodded to her and she subtly acknowledged him. They would speak later. They had been plotting their end game for some time—and she knew that their time was approaching. Was that why he was at the back of the gallery? Or was there something else? The end game, she thought, or is it a new beginning? She genuinely didn't know.

She listened to the session's final debate between two senior senators, one from the first Mars colony and the other from a planet so distant that he had to travel in cold sleep for days to get to New Omaha Beach.

She wondered at both as they danced around the obvious issue—the message from the Gateway. It was now almost a Terran year since the UDP Warrior Class Starship had disappeared and the cryptic message "BEYOND HERE LIE DREAMS" had arrived. And although its presence, its towering shadow, was everywhere, it had only been mentioned once in passing in the Senate chambers.

Danazir brought down her gavel, a delightfully tactile and anachronistic tool, to end the session. She thanked the Senators for their suggestions and promised to respond at the beginning of the next session. But even as she spoke she knew it sounded more like she was saying goodbye—and she knew it was possible that that was indeed what she was doing.

An hour later she heard a gentle knock on the secret entrance to her living quarters. Her DNA snooper had already informed her that Jedidiah was approaching—as she expected.

When she opened the door, the man standing there was not the man she had been dealing with for all these months. Well, it was the same man, but this one was clearly haunted.

"Come in Mr. Witt."

"Thank you, Madame President."

"You look—well not as well as I've seen you look, Mr. Witt."

"Indeed. That's no surprise. I'm afraid I come bearing bad news."

"*More* bad news," she corrected him.

"Indeed. May I sit Madame President, it's been a very long day and I didn't sleep last night."

"As you wish."

She watched him shamble like an old man to the chair nearest the door, then sit so heavily that she worried he would knock the seat over.

She looked closely at him but he averted his eyes. Finally he spoke, "The remark in the chamber was clever," he began.

"Yes, who would have thought her capable of such wit."

"You do know that she was quoting, don't you Madame President?"

She had not known and it surprised her. "Who. Who was she quoting?"

"A Terran congressman from the 19th Century."

Danazir thought about that then shook her head. "Can't be. All that material was lost in the Great Erasure. The Rebel Colony viral attack removed everything before 2202."

"So we have been told."

"Explain that Mr. Witt."

"S3 has controlled our history for a long time. But their control is not absolute. It has holes, creases, where the past gets through despite all of their efforts to control every bit of data in our worlds. Somehow some data evidently escaped either before or after the Great Erasure. That data managed to find its way down to us. Like this quotation and the reference to an ancient orator whose history I haven't a clue about. I do know the quote is from the 19th Century but I have no idea how I know. There are no records, but I know it to be true."

"Could that be what the ancients called intuition?"

"I can't comment on that since I don't really know the nature of that."

Danazir thought for a moment then asked, "Is this important, Mr. Witt?"

Jedidiah allowed his hands to float up in the air like two loosed doves and a look of true loss crossed his face. Finally, he spoke. "I don't know. I'm the head of your security service but I don't know. And if it was the only thing that I didn't know it wouldn't bother me but there are now so many things that I don't know—so many things."

Danazir looked closely at Jedidiah. She had trusted this man from the very first time they met and she trusted him now—and they had planned an elaborate end game together—but now she wasn't sure. "What things, Mr. Witt? What things don't you know?"

Jedidiah let out a long sigh and said, "I don't know when they will try to assassinate you. I don't know how. But I know that Cyrus can't allow you to assume any more power than you now have."

"We've talked through this before and I've taken as many precautions as I can—and you've told me how to do so. What else troubles you Mr. Witt?"

He stood and turned to the door.

"You are not to leave my presence without my permission and I do not grant you that permission."

Jedidiah turned to his President and said almost in a whisper, "They've infiltrated my entire memory system."

"What?"

"They've invaded my very being. They've changed me."

"Are you sure? How, who?"

"How, I don't know. Who, is obvious. Cyrus and S3. Somehow they entered my system and they control an entire part of who I am."

"What part?"

"Don't you understand? They've imbedded a termination date."

Danazir was suddenly speechless. All their planning had not included this possibility. Jedidiah's passing and the pre-emptive implant surgery yes—but not this. "Are you sure, Mr. Witt?"

Jedidiah nodded then a burp of laughter erupted from him. "They *want* me to know they did it. They want me to know."

"When? Not when was it imbedded, but when is the termination date?"

"That's part of their game—they made it clear that there was a termination date but they hid it so deeply in my programming that I can't possibly find it. It will just happen—like in the old days when a perfectly healthy person would suddenly keel over and die from a brain aneurysm."

Danazir thought about that and their plan. "Will it be before we begin our end game?" she asked.

He shrugged. "There's no way for me to know. Let us hope not, otherwise you will be totally on your own." He turned to go then stopped and said, "Take your normal precautions this evening, Madame President."

And then he was gone—and Danazir Yi Qal, President of the United Dominion of Planets began her nightly safety precautions feeling as alone as she'd felt when as a six-year old she'd been shipped off to a boarding school on an Independiste Indian planet.

WE DO NOT HAVE WORK/LIFE BALANCE—WE ARE INDIAN—WE WORK—PERIOD— was the motto of the school emblazoned on the decorated arches of the entry way, on the top of every assignment the school gave out, even on the sheets of her sleeping platform.

It was a lonely place for a smart girl from a modest, lower caste, Indian family whose every working dollar was spent on her tuition.

The Indian equivalent of America's 20th century's Muffies and Buffies made sure that the young Danazir never forgot the lowly station in life from which she came. As she walked down the hallways she often heard in deep dialect, "Carry your baggage, Sahib?" in mocking tones daring her to turn around and confront her abusers.

But she never did.

They short sheeted her sleeping platform so that the sheets ripped when she got into bed. They cut her hair as she slept. They slipped her hand into a pan of luke warm water as she slept to induce her to pee her bed.

But nothing could stop her from succeeding. Even the suicide of her beloved father who took his own life when he learned that an investment meant to subsidize her education had failed only set her back a day or two.

She had a duty to her family—to her caste—and she was not going to let them down.

And she didn't.

Danazir realized that she had slipped back into a moment of her past. Like the nights when she couldn't sleep because her brain insisted that she relive all the failures of her life—none of the remarkable successes—just the failures.

Then she heard her father's voice. "Move forward. The past cannot be changed, only the future can. So move forward."

She said aloud, "Right Papa. Right. The present has enough dangers without dwelling on the past."

Danazir felt it before she understood what it was.

A euphor had been activated in her body. It took her a moment to understand what was happening because as President of the United Dominion of Planets she was supposed to be free of somnambulant implants.

The tug was gentle—almost a caress. Then a gentle, female voice deep in her head, murmured. "Time to lay down your burdens, accept sleep, dear one. Then the voice became more insistent, more alluring, virtually a seduction, "Sleep. The balm that knits up the ravel'd sleeve of care."

She found herself thinking of the advice—pulling apart its meaning. Ravel'd—shouldn't it be unraveled she thought. Sleeve as in a garment of some sort—then she realized that wherever this line came from it implied a time when threads were linked together somehow to form clothing. Nothing like that had happened for hundreds of years. Clothing was not knitted. When in fact had clothing been knitted? She had no idea. Yet another fact lost during the Great Erasure.

As these thoughts rushed through her head she had a moment of clarity. Of course, they would want me to examine the statement and as I do it I will drift deeper and deeper into sleep—which is what they want!

She rose from her sleeping platform and ordered all the lights on in her bedchamber. She quickly dressed—then she saw them—creepers. Bio-products. Two lengthy ones crept beneath her bedchamber door; three rose, cobra-like from beneath her sleeping platform; one slithered down the front of her armoire; two dangled from the ceiling chandelier.

Just for a moment fear engulfed her then she remembered Jedidiah's words and calmly activated the defenses that they had so carefully planted in her bedchamber.

From her dressing closet bio-products of her own devising moved into the room—slithered—and entwined with the attacking creepers.

Looking at the twisting masses the word "lacune" flew into her head. For the briefest moment she wondered what that word meant and where it came from—then she entered her dressing closet and opened the hidden passage door.

An hour later, locked away in her safe room lodged in the ceiling—she finally found sleep—the balm that knits up the ravel'd sleeve of care.

All that now seemed so long ago. Now that they were truly at the end game. Now they were past the assassination attempts. After the surgeon had implanted the termination imbedded self of Jedidiah Witt into her chest just above her heart. After Jedidiah had been tortured and then executed by S3 even as Cyrus watched. After all that, we were finally at the end game.

She was silhouetted against the faux setting sun of New Omaha Beach as she re-watched the Holo from Moscovy in the privacy of her bed chamber. The old man floating in the air, his blood cascading down on Cyrus III of S3 who stood on the upturned pew in the ancient cathedral.

Her newly installed bedside AIU had identified the word "pew" for the bench and "cathedral" for the tall interior space. But it was Jedidiah Witt's implant next to her heart that identified Moscovy, the Rebel Colony planet, as the place and the Ancient Canary and Cyrus III as the figures in the strange death ballet.

"And the spinning man, you're sure, Mr. Witt?"

"The last of the Dream Navigators surgically gene manipulated by S3 after the Great Escaping and before the advent of Faster Than Light Speed Propulsion. We believe this dream navigator was only a child when he was sent out to find the eight escaped Dream Navigators."

"What we celebrate as the Great Escaping?"

"Yes, Madame President."

"Why do we celebrate it? Wasn't it a treasonous act?"

"Perhaps. But one of the greatnesses of the human spirit. Of bravery and inventiveness, perhaps the last of its kind—we have always celebrated that."

"Ok. And how did this last dreamer do in his mission?

"He found five of the original Dream Navigators and Cyrus had them terminated. But three were unfound," Jedidiah's implant responded.

"Walk me back a bit."

"To where?"

"The Dream Navigators were the initial explorers who allowed us to explore deep space?"

"Yes they were. After the Great Collapse that started on Mars we needed to find other habitable planets for humanity but the time it took to send explorers even in cold sleep was too long—Dream Navigators solved the problem.'

"They did indeed—and this spinning man in the cathedral is the last of them?"

"I believe so—although there are still the potential progeny of the three unfound Dream Navigators. But we have no way of knowing if the gene manipulation they went through to allow them to dream navigate was passed on to their kin.'

Danizer Yi Qal walked closer to the Holo of Cyrus III and the Canary. Finally she asked, "Why is Cyrus crying? And what does he mean by calling this man his son? We know that Cyrus was neutered along with millions of others during the Sagittarius Eclipse, the Hong Kong Event."

"As I can attest, son is a term of endearment, not necessarily an expression of biology.'

It was the first time that Jedidiah admitted that Seth may not be his biological son.

The President of the United Dominion of Planets looked out her viewing pane at the sleeping city of New Omaha Beach and for a moment was flooded by a vision of the vast, peaceful metropolis in chaos. It startled her. She had been trained from birth to believe that chaos was always the greatest enemy—but was it, she wondered. She looked up and caught the glint of the ether dome that encased the entirety of New Omaha Beach—secret scientific memos expressed concerns about an accelerating failure of the dome. And outside the dome? She asked herself—was that chaos—what was out there? Before she could fully explore the thought Jedidiah's implant supplied an answer. "Outlanders live there. They call themselves free men. They are your only hope of playing a part in the galactic drama that is already well into its second act. You need to go there—to find them—to enlist them—to fight Cyrus—they are the only ones who are untainted by the corruption of S3 controlled New Omaha Beach. They are the only ones you can potentially trust.'

She nodded. She'd known that without being told by Jedidiah's implant but it was a comfort for her to know that he agreed—but it was so dangerous, chaotic.

She turned from the viewing pane and said, "Maybe there's another way."

"There's no other way, Madame President."

"Where is Miro, our Lavolin spy?"

There was an unusual pause before the implant answered, "She didn't survive the Slave Show."

"How do we know?"

"We have the Holo.'

"Play it Mr. Witt."

Danazir, under Jedidiah's control, toggled the Holo of the Moscovy Slave Show into existence and quickly forwarded through the opening bouts –getting to Miro's almost naked entrance into the board—and the crowd's roar. She scanned forward until a moment when the Holo seemed to skip, went fuzzy, oddly out of focus.

She commanded the bedside AIU, "Cause?"

And the AIU responded, "Frequency interference.'

Jedidiah's implant cut in, "Someone trying to protect Miro.'

"Cyrus?"

"Definitely not.'

"Then who?"

"That's for us to find out.'

"But you believe that whoever tried to protect her failed to do so?"

"They definitely failed.'

Danazir looked away. "Has Miro's last comm been personalized. I want to hear her speak her thoughts."

"This is folly, Madame President. The end game is upon us. You must act.'

"I will."

"Good.'

"After I hear Miro speak. So has Miro's last comm been personalized?"

"Yes, it has. We had enough data from her other digital inputs to put together a likely recreation of her narration of the final comm she sent us.'

"Play it for me, Mr. Witt."

"Are you sure?"

"Play it Mr. Witt."

"But why – "

"Play it, Mr. Witt."

"It's heart breaking.'

"Play it, Mr. Witt."

"As you wish, Madame President.'

Using Danazir's hand Jedidiah called up the Holo of Miro's last comm.

Slowly, as if from the ether itself, Miro's image filled the Holo. As she spoke her entire body moved, somehow responding to an unheard rhythm. Her voice was light, wispy. Miro began:

TO: PRESIDENT DANAZIR YI QAL
FROM: MIRO
RE: LATEST LAVOLIN CONTACT

Cyrus's requests for Lavolin seldom surprise me but this time the request came in anger. Fury. His rage made it difficult for me to find a vein in his withered arm and by the time I managed to insert the needle's full length, his limb was slick with blood. Slowly I depressed the plunger. The journey began.

Cyrus moved fast this time. Quickly the growl of urban blight surrounded us. We had been here on the last trip so I moved back, deep in the mist and awaited the arrival of the pirate captain.

Then I sensed it. Cyrus was looking for me, hunting me. But I know many of the mist's secrets. Crouching in the entrance of the alley I folded the mist about me and stared out at the Ancient One. As long as I didn't cause ripples in the Lavolin he wouldn't find me.

Even as I was reminding myself of that, the pirate Tzu Ma Long's cruel voice echoed through the mist, "I don't care to be summoned old man. I'm not your servant."

"No, my servants obey my orders without a second command."

Tzu didn't answer but pulled back and wrapped himself in a single fold of mist. He was clearly gifted. Few learned the Lavolin's secrets so quickly.

"You have something that is mine," snapped Cyrus.

"I do have something of yours, old man." A slow smile crossed his features as he added, "Several things of yours as no doubt your sensors have told you. I know you've tracked my every step."

A silence followed. Tzu's hand gently touched the pouch on his belt. I floated closer to the two men. But it was not the two men that drew me. It was the pouch. The pouch in which a living thing spun.

Danazir paused the Holo. "This is the Dre-Rem of which you spoke, Mr. Witt?"

"Indeed Madame President.'

"And the history of the Dre-Rem?"

"Lost with all the other data in the Great Erasure viral attack against our computers in the Great War by the Rebel Colonies.'

"Why is Miro attracted to the Dre-Rem?"

"Again, without the lost data there is no way for me to know.'

"Not good enough Mr. Witt. It's a missing piece of a vast puzzle. How am I supposed to know how to act without being able to see the entirety of the picture?

"There is no complete picture from which you can act, Madame President. But act you must. Reason is no longer your best friend. You must discover as you go. Make decisions before thought. Act!'

"Did the Dre-Rem have a name? What was it called?"

"Face Dancer. It was referred to as a Face Dancer.'

"Because?"

"It was rumoured to be able to assume various forms on command. But that is not important now. Now you must act. Now! You must act!'

"Enough, Mr. Witt. Enough."

Danazir re-started the Holo. Miro's voice continued.

"Ah yes I have been following your progress," Cyrus said." Yes I have. Indeed I have." Cyrus couldn't keep the joy out of his voice. "So your raids were a success?" Cyrus's question was asked with such an obvious forced casualness that it shocked me. The Ancient One was losing his powers of control!

"My raids are always a success, old man. Talent will out in this life."

"Having the most powerful ship in the galaxy with the most advanced AIU of its kind couldn't hurt your odds of success," Cyrus barked back.

"If it pleases you to believe that it was you who invaded those planets and plundered those worlds then I will play along with your fantasy. You only watch. I do. Out in the world I do. You're no better than the audiences at slave shows. Buy the drugs, get the kick. Take the pill feel the thrill, but you never leave the safety of your comfy chair. Have it your way, it doesn't hurt me."

"You have something of mine!" Cyrus barked again.

Danazir paused the Holo again. "He's talking about those who might have the genetic alteration that could permit them to dream, isn't he Mr. Witt? The progeny of the three dreamer navigators who remained uncaptured after the Great Escaping?"

"Indeed, Madame President.'

"And what do we know of them?"

"Very little I'm afraid.'

"Can the progeny dream Mr. Witt?"

"If only we knew that -'

"But you hope they dream, assume they can dream. Surely you assume that."

"I assume nothing. Hope everything.'

"You weary me Mr. Witt."

"As I have done to many others I'm afraid.'

Danazir thought to reply, then decided against it and re-started the Holo.

"True, old one, and would you like me to deliver your property as agreed?"

"As agreed. Yes. Deliver my property as agreed."

"Send your people to the rendezvous site. I will get there when I can. I have a few chores to which I must attend first. Have your people there. Tell them to wait for me. Patience is a virtue that S3 would do well to learn."

"Deliver my property at the appointed time!"

"I command the greatest Warrior Class Starship in the galaxy! With it I can command time itself if I so wish! I will bring you what is yours when I am ready to do so. Press me more and I will consider not making the rendezvous at all. Is that clear old one?"

"Clear." It was terrible to hear the effort it took for Cyrus to admit the defeat. "Did you capture all five?"

Tzu smiled but didn't answer.

"And they are well—those on board?"

"Cold but well," the pirate chuckled. "What do you want with these five souls, old fool?"

"A curiosity. No more." Cyrus made no effort to conceal the lie.

"The UDP's latest Warrior Class Starship for an old man's curiosity? You must truly think me an idiot to believe that."

"An idiot, no. A pirate, yes." Cyrus smiled thinly then added, "So how many more did you take?"

For a moment the pirate was surprised. The serpent was old but evidently not fangless. Tzu chose to smile but once again did not respond. Then with a hard look he snapped back, "Aren't you too old for this drug stuff?"

With a delicious smile Cyrus whispered back, "One must never betray a first love. What's your first love Tzu?"

"I don't choose to confide my privacy in the likes of you, old one. Now it's time for me to return to a sober reality, something that I would suggest couldn't hurt you or your prospects for an even longer life. Don't call me again to meet you in the mist unless you have something that makes the journey worth my while. For unlike you, I am not an addict of the fog. I chart my own life course."

With that Tzu turned and moved quickly toward the mouth of the alley. I followed without thinking. But it was not him that I followed, it was the pouch at his side. I could not bear to see it move away from me. I don't know what is in the bag. All I know is that something important to me is on Tzu's belt.

Cyrus was suddenly alert and called out, "Are you in the mist too?" I stood still. He grabbed control of the mist. In an instant we were back in his rooms.

The needle was still buried deep in his vein.

I extracted the needle and raised my head. The blood from his arm had somehow soaked my smock. I literally dripped with his blood. His eyes were on me. They bored holes in my back as I moved to the door of his room. They seemed to follow me all the way to my quarters.

He knows. He must know. That is why I am sending this now without thought for my own safety. Save me if you can, Mr. Witt. If in your efforts you can bring me the contents of the bag on Tzu's belt I will be forever in your debt. I believe it has been moving toward me for a long time. That it is a giver of tears in the night and a changer of lives.

M.

Danazir walked up to the Holo and allowed her hand to grace the space that would have been Miro's cheek had Miro actually been there in the room.

Miro's Holo image turned her head as if to accept the touch then gave the slightest bow and disappeared into the infinity of Holo space.

If I had a daughter this would be she, Danazir thought then asked softly, "What happened to her?"

"Are you sure you want to see?"

"Show me, Mr. Witt."

Danazir once again found her hand in Jedidiah's control on the toggle switch of the Holo generator. The Holo paused again on the "fuzzy" section then Danazir's hand, under prompting from Jedidiah, held down all four control toggles at once. The false image produced by Mickelmast's bots disappeared and, as if from a distant horizon, the real events of Miro's end came to life.

Danazir watched in horror as the Face Dancer, transformed into a tall Russian beauty, threw Miro to the floor of the surgery then grabbed her by the throat and slammed her head into the wall—then Miro, now limp and clearly dead, was lifted by the monster-woman into a crack in the wall eight feet off the ground.

For a moment the monster looked at her deadly work then slowly with a kind of elegance transformed into a handsome young man and said as if a eulogy, "Like the hair of a horse's tail, the hair of a horse's tail.'

"Why that woman and then this young man, Mr. Witt?"

"The woman I don't know but surely you recognize the young man."

"I don't."

"You should, Madame President?"

"Why?"

"Because it's Cyrus in his prime, while he was still nothing more than a police detective.'

Danazir stared at the image before her, oddly attracted to it. "And why those words Mr. Witt? Why those words? What does he mean when he says: like the hair of a horse's tail?"

"I don't know. We've never been able to put meaning to those words.'

"Another damned mystery."

"Indeed, but there is more for you to see.'

Danazir found her fingers under Jedidiah's control reworking the toggles. The Holo skipped and they were onboard the stolen UDP starship as Raephealson leapt from the covenant deck into the deactivated zero gravity central core. His body plummeted toward the floor a full kilometer below, then suddenly stopped, eight feet off the ground, his body inverted and he began to slowly spin—his arms spread wide.

Danazir gasped, "Is he – "

"Yes, Madame President, he's in the classic Dream Navigator pose. I believe he dream navigated them to safety."

"But where, where are they now?"

After a long pause Jedidiah's implant said simply, "Playing their part, as you must.'

"It is time for me to leave the dome and enter the chaos outside, isn't it Mr. Witt?"

"Yes and the game is upon us—the end game. There is no safety here anymore, no one to trust, no one that S3 doesn't control—and the young Dreamers need your help."

Danazir turned toward the polymer pane that allowed her to see the controlled magnificence of New Omaha Beach. Then she turned her back on that world, took a deep breath and asked, "Are the Dreamers safe now?"

Chapter 2

Cas-Alta

Cas-Alta knew that the contractions would soon come more quickly. She also knew that something was wrong—very wrong.

Inside her womb the thing growing there received her anxious thought and laughed. "Oh yes, something certainly is wrong," the thing burbled as it stretched its fingers slowly in the thick liquid of its prison. It found the umbi cord and grabbed it with its fingers that had long nails that it'd bitten—yes, it already had teeth—into sharp points.

Its nails cut into the umbi cord.

Cas-Alta cried out but the Lady from the Mist put her hand over Cas's mouth and whispered, "Don't. They're looking for us. A Cossack troop passed within a quarter of a mile just a day and a half ago. And they'll be back. We covered our tracks but they're Russians so they're good hunters and will figure it out soon. So, no noise."

Cas nodded and turned her attention inward. She felt the baby's finger nails on the umbi cord and gently stretched it away from him—she knew it was a him—had known it from the moment the pirate raped her. The pirate who was, unbeknownst to Tzu Ma Long, one of his whore mother's many unwelcomed children.

Inside the thing—the boy—felt the umbi cord pulling away from him and cursed, "Bitch!" He turned to the wall of his prison and inserted one long index finger nail and was rewarded with a gush of blood. The crimson mixed with the almost clear fluid of his prison and he drank it deeply—and smiled. So be it, he thought. Born again, fine, your choice not mine, but this time I'll make you pay—I'll make all of you pay.

The Face Dancer watched the welt rise on Cas's abdomen and saw the rush of blood from her birth canal. "We have to work fast now, so take a breath and then push."

The thing—the boy—well let's be honest—the Antigen—scraped his sharp finger nail across Cas-Alta's womb a second time and gloried in the pain he caused. Then he felt the strong push of the contraction forcing him toward the birth canal. He put his hands above his head like a diver and thought, Why the fuck not, let's go again.

The Antigen came out in a whoosh of blood, mucus and cord that quickly coated the Face Dancer's hands and face. When she wiped it out of her eyes, she turned and saw a sight she thought she'd never see—the "baby" was standing on the stone floor of the cave, his eyes wide open, a full head of hair and long finger nails—and most disconcerting—a large erect penis and a knowing smile. He strode across the stone floor and, before the Face Dancer could stop him, he grabbed the scalpel she had used to perform an episiotomy on Cas.

"Don't worry," the Antigen said, "as you can see I'm no ordinary baby." He leaned over and spat a string of mucus from his mouth then covered one nostril and blew the gunk from the other as he raised the scalpel and in one stroke cut the umbi cord and quickly tied his end. "Wouldn't want to go where she's going, now would I?" The Face Dancer leapt forward.

"I had to cut her to allow—you—now she's bleeding and could bleed to death."

"Could she now?"

What was that accent, she wondered as she looked to Cas-Alta who was already turning a ghastly shade of pale. "Your mother could die."

"She just carried me, that's all. I'm the polar opposite of you. You're a Dre-Rem—I destroy you and yours."

"Yes."

"Yes, what?"

The Face Dancer had no answer. "Don't hurt her. She gave birth to you. She's your mother."

"She did nothing more than force me back into existence and besides Antigens don't have mothers."

"An Antigen? That's what you are?"

"Yes, and she must have known that long ago but she's such a selfish whore. Who cares what happens to her?"

In a gush the after birth emerged and slid to the floor. Before the Lady from the Mist could react, the Antigen grabbed the nutrient rich mesh and consumed it in three long swallows.

While he was busy eating, the Face Dancere glanced again at Cas-Alta and wondered if the healer would survive. The cave floor was already sticky with her blood and there was no way to replenish what had been lost. Then the Face Dancer noticed Cas-Alta's eyes moving quickly beneath her closed eyelids and she knew that the healer had retreated to the world of dreams.

The Antigen shoved the Face Dancer aside and lifted Cas-Alta's eye lids—then he smiled.

"Watch this, you witch." He leaned in close to Cas-Alta's left ear and screamed, "Dream no more, dream no more, dream—forever."

Instantly Cas-Alta's eyes stopped moving. A look of desperate loss crossed her face.

"The room, I lost the dream room."

The Antigen hopped on one foot and laughed loudly – "Not lost, whore, not lost—have been expelled from—kicked out of—never to find it again—ever." Then the naked Antigen grabbed a towel and wiped himself clean. Finished, he threw the towel at the Face Dancer and said, "It's been a slice. That Gateway you're all aiming for—well it's my role to close that fucking thing, like I closed the whore's access to dreaming. I'll close the Gateway— forever, forever."

Then he leapt at the Face Dancer and stuck his tongue deep down her throat and hissed, "What a cunting thing you are."

Then he was gone—if it wasn't for all the blood and Cas-Alta's obvious pain the Face Dancer would have thought this was some peculiar trick of the light—but she knew the stories—of Antigens—of creatures in the night who stole babies and planned the rack and ruin of worlds—and were directly involved in the killing of dreams. As a Dre-Rem herself she knew that this creature was her sworn enemy—but also, somehow, a relation. A twisted cousin, an evolutionary reaction to the death of dreams.

The Face Dancer knelt beside Cas-Alta and gently pushed back her short hair from her forehead. Leaning in close to her ear she whispered, "Can you heal yourself?"

"Don't know," came the rasped response.

"Can I heal you? If I become you, can I heal you?"

Cas-Alta forced her head back and forth, tears came to her eyes, "It would kill you."

The Face Dancer stood and thought of her life—her confinement, her required obedience to whoever held the box—her origins as a Dre-Rem on the outer rings of Saturn—of Legolas, her creator, her one love who had made her a Face Dancer to keep her safe—and knew—had known all along that it could end like this. It almost made her smile.

She stared down at Cas-Alta and slowly became a mist then transformed into an exact replica of the healer.

Carefully she helped Cas-Alta to a standing position—doing so caused the healer to whimper in pain and another gush of blood filled her skirts. Then the Face Dancer held her and began to rock her—back and forth, back and forth and a rhythm came from her lips—a rhythm in frequencies she had never heard before—there was a young cowboy who lived on the range, his horse and his cattle were his only companions—and she continued to rock the healer —and as she did she felt her own life ebbing.

If seen from a distance they appeared to be a woman in a mirror—slowly dancing in a far-off cave.

The Face Dancer took a deep breath then allowed her hands to roam Cas-Alta's body—and everywhere they touched they found pain that she took upon herself. Cas-Alta began to protest but the Face Dancer was stronger and held her up and explored—deeper and deeper—her head flung back, pain etching its gruesome masterpiece on her face. And then she let go.

Cas-Alta felt herself enveloped, inside a slowly spinning world—spinning, spinning—coming back to life.

When she opened her eyes, she found herself staring into the hardened face of a teenager—a teenaged boy she'd given birth to only hours before. She went to rise but found herself partially pinned beneath the Face Dancer. Then she heard a sharp click and looked at the teenager again. He held the ancient Russian box from which the Face Dancer had arisen.

"In!" he commanded. "I said get in the box, you're far too weak to resist an Antigen. Get back in your prison. You are nothing more than a Face Dancer. A toy. In!"

The Face Dancer whined only once, then she left the form of Cas-Alta and became a mist—and with a single swirl—a last dance of freedom—she entered the box at the teenager's belt.

He snapped it shut, then turned to Cas-Alta – "You aren't long for this world "mom" – why not end it now and be done with this awful existence."

He tossed the scalpel to her. She allowed it to bounce off her leg and clink on the stone floor.

"There's nothing awful in life, son."

"I'm not your son. I'm your death."

"No, you are my son and will always be my son."

The Antigen turned on his heel. He was already a young, strong man — as he left the cave he laughed a thin laugh—and in a moment, he and his laugh and the Face Dancer—were gone.

The next morning Cas-Alta awoke and struggled to her feet. She wobbled there for several minutes until some sense of balance returned to her.

Her memory was fuzzy. She knew that she had given birth—that the thing she had birthed was a thing rather than a human.

It was a thing that had a name; a much-feared name: Antigen.

The very thought sent a shiver through her entire being and she had to go down on all fours to regain control of herself.

She knew that she'd given birth to that which can destroy everything she'd ever found of value.

Pain began to rise in her and for a moment she longed to just lie on the ground and sleep and hopefully drift to her dream room—but then she remembered. The Antigen, her son, had shut the access point to her dream room—locked her permanently out of it—and he had laughed at her attempts to get in.

The word "alone" came up in her and she forced herself to ignore it and look her present circumstances squarely in the face.

She was in a cave, on a Russo Rebel Colony—a place that killed Miro. Her fellow Dreamers were nowhere to be seen. They must have left her, she thought. It would be the wise thing to do. She forced down the panic that thought brought. She made herself recall Elijah Jasper and his command to her: be brave.

She said the word aloud: brave. Then she added the word: smart.

"Think clearly, now what exactly are my circumstances," she said aloud—then she enumerated them—no clothes except the blood-stained skirts she was wearing, no money, no identity papers, no food, weak from childbirth, miles from Moscovy and the Russo version of cold outside.

Every journey begins with a single step she quoted to herself although she didn't know the source of the quote.

So, she began—one step outside the cave—the birth cave—and she felt the early dawn sun on her face—and allowed herself to smile.

By noon she had managed to find the main transport artery but had to guess which direction to head. She assumed one direction would lead to Moscovy—the other to who knew where.

She decided to walk toward the sun. Fifty steps then a ten-count halt—then another fifty steps.

She allowed herself to leave the transit way as the sun dipped suddenly beneath the horizon. She walked back toward a tall stand of birch trees, and for a moment marvelled at their slender beauty. Beneath them she found groves of mushrooms. She looked at them carefully and finally decided which variety was probably safe. She realized that it didn't matter all that much. She was weak from exertion and hadn't eaten in days—starving was a real possibility.

She reached down and gently removed the cap of a large mushroom. She allowed her incredible powers of observation to move forward and examined the fungus. Tiny yellow dots on the underside, a rim of some sort of purple around the circumference, spores beneath. All good she thought as she moved it toward her lips. Then she saw it—the tiniest worm she'd ever seen—but it had a crest around its head—poison.

She dropped the thing and found herself crying, hysteria rising fast in her as she ran and ran and ran.

She actually tripped over them—wild beets. She quickly examined the plant and took a large bite—her entire body reacted to the glory of the vegetable.

That night she ate her fill and found in the morning that she had more strength than she had the day before.

She made her way back to the transit way and was surprised to see what she assumed were emergency vehicles racing back the way from which she had come. She reasoned that they could only be going to Moscovy—perhaps to help with those hurt by Mickelmast's explosives after the Great and Grand Slave Show.

As they passed in a screeching caravan she examined them—those driving were swarthy men—Asiatics—she assumed that the medical services in Moscovy had been over-matched by the number of injured and Moscovy had called to the hinterland for more assistance.

So she retraced her footsteps and found that by day's end the onion domes of Moscovy rose on the far horizon.

As the faux stars of the planet's ether dome came out she entered the great sprawl of Moscovy.

It was then that the ether dome gave away her presence.

"Don't move. Prepare for DNA reading. Don't move!"

The disembodied voice came from every direction and the people all around her backed off and stared at her.

She was near an underground transit way so without a second thought she raced down the stairs into the crowd waiting there. There were several platforms and the voice boomed again, "Don't move. Present your papers, now!" She ducked into a side stairway heading downward. At the bottom of the stairway she saw a sleeping old woman in a booth, her head resting against the polymer pane. She snored loudly. There was a sign in the window of the booth in the Intergalactic Tongue: "Don't ask me questions."

Ok, no questions, she thought. She tore off her blood-soaked outer skirt and stuffed it into the back of the booth. If the ether dome was tracking DNA then it might, for a moment, be attracted to the skirt.

She raced down an escalator that seemed to go on forever and hopped onto the first transit unit that arrived.

At the first stop she saw many uniformed personnel and for a moment looked for a place to hide then she realized they weren't law enforcement officers, they were medical people.

She stepped out just as the doors were closing and followed them into a huge building that she assumed was some sort of facility to help the sick and injured.

It was chaos. The injured and dying were everywhere—on benches, on chairs, on the floor.

She followed the medical personnel and grabbed a doctor's robe as she moved behind them. Putting it on pleased her as her bloody skirts were covered by the gown.

At a junction the medical personnel headed left and she went to the right.

"Doctor!" The voice was female and urgent.

Cas-Alta stopped and turned toward the voice. It was a young woman. Because she was carrying files Cas Alta assumed that she was a nurse of some sort.

An odd look crossed the nurse's face.

"Are you here to help with the emergency patients?" the young woman asked.

Cas nodded.

"Good. Some people don't like foreign doctors, personally I don't give a damn, a doctor is a doctor." She handed Cas the files and said, "This way. That room has already been triaged."

They turned a corner and there before them was a massive room filled with more of the injured—these clearly more critical than the ones in the other room. As they moved through the large room Cas was distracted by the sound of a woman's keening cry in a small room off to one side.

"What's this?" Cas asked.

"Just a palliative room—a place for the final passing."

Cas gave the files back to the nurse and entered the palliative room and before the nurse could complain she slammed the door shut—then locked it.

Once she did, a beautiful middle-aged woman turned to her. The etchings of grief were on her fine features—tears in her eyes—a great weariness about her.

"Are you a doctor?" she asked

Cas nodded.

"They said it was hopeless and they sent us here."

It was only then that Cas saw the terribly mangled body of a little girl.

She took a step toward her. "What–?"

"The explosion. She was right beneath a lamp post when it -"

Cas felt sick. The explosions that Mickelmast had set as a diversion to allow them to escape had dropped the pole and hundreds of shards of cement and glass onto this poor little girl. Cas took a breath and for a moment checked herself. Was she strong enough? It didn't matter. They had caused this in their effort to find another gifted person—and their efforts had ended up terribly injuring this innocent little girl.

She looked at the hurt girl. So different from the Antigen I gave birth to, she thought, so different.

She approached the girl noting each injured part of the poor child. Cas didn't notice the girl's mother step to one side or the insignia on her shoulder.

She started with the most serious of the wounds—it took over two hours—but by the end she was able to turn to the mother and say, "I think, with luck, she'll be ok."

The woman crossed herself several times and before Cas could stop her, embraced the healer in a bear hug that almost took what little strength Cas had left from her.

Just as Cas was extricating herself from the hug the door of the small room crashed open and three burly guards pointed a DNA decoder at Cas and said, "Stand back from these citizens. Show us your papers."

Cas found herself drooping and would have fallen to the floor had the woman with the insignia not grabbed her beneath the arms and held her up.

"This doctor saved my daughter's life."

"We need to check her DNA."

"You need to check nothing. Don't you know who I am? Can you not see the insignia on my shoulder?"

"Yes—but—

"No but. This woman is a hero and I will see that she is treated as such. Now get out. Now!"

The three guards exchanged looks then backed out of the room.

The woman shut the door and turned to Cas. She lit some bio product and inhaled the smoke from it. She let the smoke out in a long thin line and finally said, "So who are you exactly?"

Cas awakened two days later in a bed with fresh sheets and the sweet smell of basil and rosemary. She carefully got to her feet and looked out the large bedroom window—birch trees.

"Nice to see you up and about."

Cas whirled around and almost fainted from the effort. The woman from the hospital was sitting in a large chair. Her daughter slept in a small bed beside her. A thickly furred feline of some sort slept at her feet.

"Thank you." Cas couldn't think of anything else to say.

"You saved my daughter's life." The statement was flat. There wasn't gratitude, just a statement of fact. "And you don't have the ID necessary to allow you to enter Moscovy." Another flat statement of fact.

Cas held her breath.

"And more seriously your DNA doesn't match Russo requirements."

Cas continued her silence.

"Were you one of the terrorists who planted the bombs in our city?"

It took Cas a moment to understand the term terrorist. When she did, it appalled her—but then of course, from the Moscovy perspective that was exactly what they were.

"Don't answer that. I don't want to know. I want to think of you only as the doctor who saved my daughter." She glanced down at the sleeping girl.

"How is she?" Cas asked.

"She'd better be fine or I'll report you to the authorities. Do you understand me?"

Cas nodded.

"You'll stay on the dacha grounds. Any attempt to leave the dacha grounds and the cuff on your ankle will be activated and you'll die a particularly nasty death. That will happen if you try to leave. If my daughter dies you'll wish you'd died that death—because if she dies your death will make that look like a fate much to be desired. Clear?"

Cas didn't move.

"Up and down means yes."

The feline awakened and stretched then eyed Cas with open malevolence—then hissed.

Cas backed off a step then moved her head slowly—up and down.

The next day, Cas carefully opened the door of her patient's room. The little girl was moving fitfully beneath a heavy blanket as her body dealt with the pain that Cas's ministrations couldn't stop from sprouting in various parts of the poor girl's body. To one side was an iron bedside table that, if Cas was back home, would have been filled with herbal medications from her garden. But now the heavy thing was a perch for the large feline thing who hissed at Cas.

She leaned against the wrought iron table and put her hand to the girl's forehead. It was no surprise that her palm found considerable heat there. Infection, she thought, but where exactly was it? She had carefully removed the shrapnel pieces from Mickelmast's diversionary incendiary devices and bathed the wounds in the curative herbs she insisted her mother get for her.

Yet there was still fever.

She bent close to the girl and whispered her name into her ear. The girl roused for a moment then returned to her troubled sleep. For an instant Cas thought she saw eye movement beneath the girl's lids. "Could this one be dreaming?" But on closer inspection she found what she thought she'd find: eyelashes had fallen into the girl's eyes and they were autonomically moving to try and be rid of them.

Cas took a clean edge of her apron and, opening the eye lid with one hand, dabbed away the offending lashes with the other. The soporific she had administered just an hour ago stopped the girl from waking.

Just to be sure she touched the back of her hand to the girl's forehead a second time—the heat was certainly still there. The furry feline reached over and scraped a sharp claw along Cas' hand, drawing five crimson lines of blood. Cas withdrew her hand as the feline licked it's paw as if she enjoyed the taste of Cas' blood.

Cas stepped back and looked at the girl from a distance. She allowed her remarkable ability to focus to move forward. The hair of the girl's bangs was fine but splintered more than it should have been. And her skin was oddly bad for someone so young. Pustules on the side of her nose and what could be the beginning of a goiter on the girl's throat.

She stepped toward the girl.

The feline hissed again.

"Scat," Cas said as she flicked a side of the sheet at the furry thing. The feline retreated to beneath the girl's bed.

Cas sat on the bed and gently moved the girl into a sitting position then crawled in behind her, her legs outside the girl's, her arms around the girl's chest—then she took a deep breath and moved forward into her facial bones.

Something leapt from the girl and tried to enter Cas. Just in time Cas threw the girl from her.

Cold sweat coated Cas's face as she realized two things at once. First was that the girl was not sick from the shrapnel, but there was something already at work hollowing out the girl—and that that something was alive—as alive and vicious as the Antigen she's given birth to.

Second, that had the alive thing entered her, it would surely have killed her.

She sensed the door of the room opening—and a third reality hit her. She might never be able to cure this girl and that being the case she would never be free of this party member, who now stood in the doorway, her arms across her chest, a scowl on her face.

Cas realized what this scene must look like. She on the bed, the girl thrown violently to one side.

"Is this some sort of new treatment? It had better be –

Cas took a breath and tried to steady herself. "She has fever." She didn't mention infection... or the thing.

"And this," the party member said indicating her daughter half on and half off the bed, "is some sort of treatment?"

For a moment Cas wanted to tell this woman the truth—your daughter may soon need to be moved to the room of great passing—assuming they had such on Muscovy.

The girl began to scream—and her screams seemed like glass shards piercing both healer and mother.

The mother went to the girl and was about to throw her arms around her when Cas Alta grabbed her and pulled her away.

"What! How dare you—

"The disease is alive in her and would gladly leap to you."

"The disease?"

"It's alive. It might have entered through her wounds or been there all along, lain dormant until her body was too weak to fight it. But now it's ascending, growing even as we speak. And it's strong. Maybe too strong even for me. It would kill you quickly then try to return to her—she's the original host."

The mother's hand flew to her mouth stifling a scream and rage crossed her hardened features.

"And you can't—

"No. I don't know. It may be her time of passing."

"No!"

"Yes. I'm sorry, but we are all human and we all must pass."

Just for a moment compassion bloomed on the party woman's face—then her hardness returned. "I'm going to lock this door. In ten hours I'm going to return. If only one of you is alive when I re-open this door it had better be my daughter and not you. Have I made myself clear? Take it upon yourself and don't let it return to its host—to my daughter—am I perfectly clear?"

Cas nodded.

The door slammed shut—a dead bolt slammed into place with a dull thud.

Cas took a quick look at the girl on the bed then turned her attention to the corners of the room mindful to keep her distance from the girl—and the disease that lurked there.

The bars on the window attracted her attention. But in ten hours with no tools she knew that she couldn't even begin to loosen them or open the bolted door so she slowly turned her gaze back to the girl and spoke sharply, "Wake up. If we don't fight this thing together we both die. Is that clear? Wake up!"

The girl's eyes slowly opened and she pulled the heavy blanket up to her chin.

Cas quickly moved to the bed and shook her hard. The girl spat at her.

Good, Cas thought. You'll need to be angry to fight this thing. For a moment she longed to be back in her garden—where she understood how things worked and why they were where they were. Where things had a discernable order.

Her thoughts were interrupted by the girl's projectile vomit that splatted with remarkable force against the far wall.

Her body's trying to fight, Cas thought—then she saw the feline creep out from beneath the bed and begin to slurp up the vomit—and an idea bloomed in Cas' head—not a nice idea—but the only one that wouldn't result in either her or the girl dying in this very room.

"What do you call the creature?" Cas demanded.

The girl mumbled something.

"Come on, tell me its name."

"Hecuba."

"Will it come if you call for it?"

"I don't know."

"Yes, you do. Answer me. Will it come if you call it?"

"Yes."

"Good," Cas said. Then she looked around the room for something to cage Hecuba. Nothing came to mind so she reached over and grabbed the blanket from the girl who howled a complaint and reached for her arm.

Cas easily avoided her then realized that it was the disease reaching for her, not the girl.

The feline belched then lifted a leg and urinated beside the vomit.

What little hesitation Cas had vanished at that moment.

"Move to the side of the bed." The girl stared at her. "Do it!" Cas demanded.

The girl slowly moved to the far side of the bed and rested her back against the wall there.

"Good," Cas said as she readied the thick blanket and sat on the far side of the bed. "Are you ready?" Cas asked.

"For what?"

"To call your pet."

"Why would I—

"Because you want to live and so do I. Are you ready?"

"I guess."

"Good, now turn toward me."

The girl did.

Cas readied the thick blanket between them. "Now call Hecuba."

The girl did in a low whisper and the fat thing slowly moved toward the bed and hopped up. It turned to Cas and hissed loudly. Then settled on the softest part of the heavy blanket.

Cas nodded.

The feline hissed again.

Cas turned to the girl and said slowly, "Raise your right hand—and arm." The girl did. "Good, now watch where I move my hand. Do you see it—right over my heart."

"I see it."

"Good—now take a deep breath and reach for my heart."

The girl took a breath then reached across the bed to Cas.

Then the girl felt it—the thing deep inside her raced up her arm and into her hand.

Cas saw it too—and just as it leapt for her—she reached down to the blanket and threw the feline between herself and the thing from the girl.

The feline gave a shriek as the thing entered her. Just for an instant it looked at Cas clearly wanting to demand—did you do this?

Then in one quick motion Cas grabbed the corners of the blanket and tied then tightly about Hecuba—who was already transforming into something even more hideous than it was before as the disease took hold inside the animal.

"Grab the other corner!" Cas demanded.

The girl did just in time to stop Hecuba's effort to escape but not in time to avoid Hecuba's sharp claws that lanced out at her and cut her deeply on the arm.

The girl let out a screech.

Cas ignored the girl and leapt for the loose corner—tying the thing tight before Hecuba could figure out that there was another way out. Then grabbing the sheets off the bed, she tied those around the blanket. Hecuba—or the thing inside Hecuba—howled protests and the girl began to cry.

"Let her go!" the girl screamed over and over again.

Then Cas did the only thing she could think of doing—she grabbed the iron bedside table—and smashed it down over and over again on the bundled thing inside the blanket—until there was no movement or protest.

Until she and girl were safe from the thing.

I've taken a life, Cas thought. I am now a person who has taken a life—no matter how hideous and diseased—I've taken a life.

"Was she now a terrorist?" she asked herself as she turned to the girl and ministered to her badly cut arm.

Chapter 3

The Dreamers

While Cas was committing the first act of violence in her life on the Russo Rebel Colony planet, Raephealson was inside a deep cave far away on the Independentiste planet of New K-Bek.

This cave's ancient wall drawings, prehistoric scribblings, drew him like an oasis does a desert traveler. The others, Sun Tu, Kelt and Mickelmast were busily exploring what they assumed was a basic Franco planet.

Raephealson's fingers traced the delicate lines of the ancient sketches. He didn't know the names of the animals that were being hunted although he assumed they were being killed for the festival of the Great Escaping.

"You like the drawings?"

Raephealson whirled around to see a bearded older man, who then repeated his question. Raephealson didn't understand a word the man said. The bearded man stepped forward and extended his hand in which he held a small flimsie. "If you like these," he said indicating the cave drawings, "then you'll love my daughter's peinture." He pointed to the small flimsie and added, "Come visit us at that address. My name's Moreau. My daughter's paintings have great stories too. It's the stories of these cave drawings that you like, isn't it?" Then the bearded man farted loudly, smiled broadly and left Raephealson alone in the cave.

Raephealson didn't know what to do so he turned back to the sketches on the cave walls.

The bearded man was wrong. It was not the stories that drew Raephealson. It was something else. That something else he thought of as "the reaching." Not Holos or even flat faces, both of which were merely accurate depictions of their subjects, ever touched Raephealson. But these simple lines ignored accuracy and "reached" for essence—the beating heart of their subjects—and their reachings profoundly touched Raephealson.

Raephaelson approached the largest etching and was about to touch the lines, when the card the old man had put in his hand fell to the floor. Raephaelson looked down at it and wondered what the writing on it meant—then he looked at the etching—a four-legged mammal of some sort pursued by men with long sticks—and for a moment he felt the great beast's pain as one of the hunter's sticks entered its body and the great beast began the death travel, as his grandda had done so long ago.

About a kilometer from Raephealson's cave, by the side of an almost deserted transit way, Sun Tu finally addressed what had been on all their minds. "We abandoned Cas-Alta!" she said.

"We did what we needed to do to stay alive," Kelt stated.

"You're a coward!" she said.

"Now, you're being a fool," Kelt responded.

"No—now we're trying to find someone who can fix Mama," Mickelmast interjected. "Without Mama we'll never get Cas back; without her—well I'd say we're lost but I know where we are—so –

"Mickelmast we get what you're trying to say," Sun Tu snarked.

"How much longer can your bots duplicate what Mama does?" Kelt asked.

"I'm amazed they've managed as much as they have," Mickelmast said, "but every time we go back to them, they'll give us less. If they were human I'd say they're getting tired."

Sun Tu kicked the ground then looked at the two men and said another thought that they were all thinking, "Like Raephealson, tired like Raephealson."

The men nodded.

"From Mama's last bio readings of him I'm pretty sure that he will not survive another effort to dream navigate. It will kill him," Mickelmast said.

That sat in the air like something fat and heavy—and all three, even without Mama's bio readings, knew that it was true—although none of them could explain exactly how they knew.

"Where is he?" asked Kelt.

"Back at that cave with those drawings he seems to like. I put a bot transmitter on him so we know exactly where he is," Mickelmast said.

"Good," said Sun Tu.

"But we have to fix Mama. She failed. We don't know exactly why she failed but she did. And we have to address that—now," Mickelmast stated.

"I'm open to suggestions," said Sun Tu.

"Well we're not going to find what we need out here in the sticks. We'll have to chance going into town—New K-Bec City."

"Let's at least let Mama help us with that. It shouldn't take much computing power—contact her, Mickelmast," said Sun Tu.

The portly boy shrugged then tapped the shunt in his neck. "How you feeling Mama?"

"Peachy. Just peachy." Then the great thinking thing snapped off the connection not unlike a petulant child whose personal comm had been confiscated by a parent.

Mickelmast threw up his hand and gave the international signal for "I gave it my best."

But Sun Tu wasn't buying it. "Try again."

"She doesn't like to be bothered."

"Well we don't like traveling in a United Dominion of Planets warrior class starship without a functioning AIU. Try her again."

Mickelmast looked to Kelt for support but found none there, just a whispered, "You heard the lady, try again."

In Mickelmast's book he comments on this moment thusly: *Caught! Oh faithful droogies—caught between two strong droogettes. Has that ever happened to you? I've periodically thought of a certain body part caught between two strong droogettes—a fate devoutly to be wished for— but this was not like that. Not at all. Between us—just between us, entrenouses—I felt a wee bit trapped—and not in that happy way. But your daring narrator proceeded against all the female odds. Despite the Amazons I moved bravely forward.*

"I said try again," the EnterPren princess demanded.

"Ok," Mickelmast said. He activated his shunt and in a high sweet voice said, "Knock, knock."

A "ding-a-ding-ding" filled the air and Mama came back on line, "Ok so listen up cause this is how this is going down – "

"Anything you want Mama."

"Shut up! Here it is—see if you can follow. I'm the wicked old witch and you are a fat kid knocking on my cookie house door."

Kelt mouthed "What the fuck's she talking about?"

"Ok fatso, you got the rules?"

"Sure, Mama, good rules."

"You betcha. So you start again—go ahead I haven't got all day."

Sun Tu mouthed "knock, knock" and Mickelmast tentatively said, "Knock, knock."

Mama immediately answered, "Who's there?"

"It's your dear Hippo, Mama."

"Dear Hippo who?"

Mickelmast looked at Sun Tu but she didn't have any advice so Mickelmast tried, "Your dear Hippo who just wants to know how you are."

"Peachy—you've already asked that—peachy, wie sucks man Peachy?"

Kelt muttered, "Wie sucks what?"

"It's old German –" but before Mickelmast could explain more he was stopped by a high-pitched moan coming from Mama. It stunned the three Dreamers.

Finally Kelt asked, "Is she crying? Fuck our AIU is crying!"

"Lost, lost, lost," Mama screamed, "the centre cannot hold. No, can't. Centre can't hold."

"Which centre, Mama, tell Hippo which centre."

But she was shouting, "Medic! Medic! I need a medic!" Then, without segue, she enacted 107 death scenes in just under three minutes ending with the death aria from La Traviata. None of which the three Dreamers could even take a guess at identifying. At the end of the recitation she repeated, "The centre cannot hold, the centre cannot hold, the centre cannot hold." Then very loudly she screamed, "Medic –" then repeated it 47 times each an exact .23 decibel softer than the one before—until she was "gone.'

Sun Tu turned to Mickelmast and demanded, "Have you ever heard an AIU act like that?"

"No, but Mama is no ordinary AIU."

"And that calling for a medic—what the hell's a medic?"

Sun Tu unfolded a pocket monitor and was already scanning thousands of words as they flew past her—suddenly she stopped and said, "Medic, a non-doctor who treats soldiers on the battlefield. Medic."

The three looked at each other and finally Kelt asked, "What's a non-doctor?"

"And what was all that melodrama?" demanded Sun Tu.

"They must be samplings from things in her memory banks," Mickelmast answered but he was clearly being evasive.

"But how did those things get into her memory banks?" Sun Tu asked—no, demanded.

"I don't know," Mickelmast admitted.

"Those are things from before the Great Erasure, aren't they?" Kelt asked.

"How could that be? These self evolving AIU's weren't invented until well after the erasure," Sun Tu pressed.

"Then how – "Kelt began.

"I don't know," Mickelmast admitted a second time.

But now Sun Tu wasn't listening to Mickelmast. She had entered a new search term and was scanning data sheets, hundreds a minute.

"What are you doing?" Kelt demanded.

"She said the centre will not hold."

"So?"

"So, I made a mistake once and slept with an EntrePren Specule, a handsome Specule."

"How was he?" Kelt asked with a smile.

"Pedestrian, significantly less imaginative than I'd hoped."

"So again I ask, so what?" Mickelmast broke in.

"So he liked doing a thing he called reciting a thing he called poems."

"And the line "the centre cannot hold" is one of the lines from that poem thing?"

Like this?" Mickelmast blurted out as rows and rows of words appeared on the screen. "That thing? That poem thing that Mama repeated?

The three stared at the screen and read the knowledge of William Butler Yeats from a period so long ago that they didn't even have a name for it:

THE SECOND COMING

Turning and turning in the widening gyre
The falcon cannot hear the falconer;
Things fall apart; the centre cannot hold;
Mere anarchy is loosed upon the world,
The blood-dimmed tide is loosed, and everywhere
The ceremony of innocence is drowned;
The best lack all conviction, while the worst
Are full of passionate intensity.
Surely some revelation is at hand;
Surely the Second Coming is at hand.
The Second Coming! Hardly are those words out
When a vast image out of Spiritus Mundi
Troubles my sight:

The writing suddenly vanished and Mama recited the rest of the poem in what could only be called a booming, if oddly neutral, voice:

a waste of desert sand;
A shape with lion body and the head of a man,
A gaze blank and pitiless as the sun,
Is moving its slow thighs, while all about it
Wind shadows of the indignant desert birds.
The darkness drops again but now I know
That twenty centuries of stony sleep
Were vexed to nightmare by a rocking cradle,
And what rough beast, its hour come round at last,
Slouches toward Bethlehem to be born?

The three Dreamers looked at each other. No one knew what to say.

Returning to the cave, they found Raephealson still staring at the odd etchings on the walls. It seemed to Sun Tu, Mickelmast and Kelt that Raephealson had hardly moved a muscle from where they left him several hours before.

"What does he see in them?" Sun Tu asked.

"Ghosts," Kelt snarked.

"Or dreams of ghosts," Mickelmast said with a surprisingly calm note in his voice.

"What does that mean?" Kelt said dismissively.

Sun Tu carefully approached the Heavy Worlder and placed a cool hand to his face, "What do you see, Raephealson, tell me. They're just bad drawings of mammals that no longer exist."

Raephealson shook his large head and managed, "More, more."

"More what?" Sun Tu asked gently.

Raephealson showed her the small flimsie the old man had given him. Her translator quickly read it. The written word of New K-Bek was no problem for the translator although some of the idioms didn't translate very well. "It's a home that sells things, Raephealson."

Raephealson took a long breath and sought the words he needed. Finally he said, "Go there. Have to go there."

Sun Tu looked at Mickelmast. "After we look to Mama. Without her we're stuck here."

Raephealson repeated, "Go there. Have to go there."

"OK, Raephealson we'll go there—but later. After we look after Mama."

"Come on," Kelt said, "we have a long way to go and it's already late afternoon."

It took all of Sun Tu, Kelt and Mickelmasts' strengths to get Raephealson to move him toward the trans terminal.

As they made their way Mickelmast instructed his bots to form the Richards (pronounced REE-shards, the local currency) necessary to purchase their transit tickets.

Standing at the transit platform Raephealson's mind searched the images he'd seen on the cave walls, not to accurately reproduce them but to see through them—to the dream behind them—to which they led—that to which the paintings "reached" —— to the other side.

Entry B—from the Diary of the Suicided Man

—The Sagittarius Eclipse

(No Date was recorded for this entry)

And then there was the event we so charmingly named the Sagittarius Eclipse.

Deus! We are never so fucked as when we fuck ourselves—either some philosopher said that or some philosopher should have said that.

Well be that as it may, the Sagittarius Eclipse took place in Hong Kong on Deep Water Road in the Wan Chen district.

One of my many spies sent a report that Olya had been located and was going to be in Hong Kong—Olya. So when the call came in that there was an illegal hardwiring taking place in real time in Hong Kong, I made myself available. I fucked myself.

Or had she lured me to Hong Kong so I'd be the one who got the S3 call to go to Deep Water Bay Road? I don't know—and yes, I care—but I don't know.

Well, the ultra rich neighbours of the condo had reported unearthly screams coming from the penthouse of their building so S3 broke through the protective firewall and detected the illegal hardwiring.

By the time I arrived at the one hundred and forty-seven storey condo everyone from the building was on the street wearing face masks, some with elaborate mouth and nose filters. I could only see their eyes but they looked scared—no, they looked haunted.

Then out came the hazmat suits. Hundreds of them—and as the crowd slipped on the suits they became ghosts standing in groups in the twilight in the middle of Deep Water Road.

At this point I didn't know about the contagion that would neuter the entire island and cause it and its residents to be removed from the face of the planet—with extreme prejudice. Nuclear prejudice.

Some said it was the only way to stop the contagion. Some said we did the Hong Kongers a favour saving them from the horrors they would have faced had they lived. I don't know—and no, I don't know why I didn't get sick—I just got old—very old, very fast.

But I'm ahead of myself.

I'll never forget stepping out of the private gold-plated elevator that serviced the penthouse and the sudden cold—an unearthly cold since we had controlled our climate for almost two and a half centuries by that point. It was a warning. Nature's warning. But of course I ignored it.

Taking the key the concierge had given me I inserted the twelve pronged thing into the lock—and felt a powerful force within—and I heard the voice inside my head screaming at me to run, to run far and fast. And of course I ignored it—as I always had—up until that day.

I threw open the door and was stunned by what awaited me there—no, assaulted me there.

All four walls of the vast living space were seamless monitors, as were the ceiling and the floor.

And the maniacal image of Kar the Dreamer leapt from one to the next—but it wasn't him or his hysterical laughter and obscene commands that drew my attention.

As a police officer for many years I thought I was inured to crime scenes but this was not a crime scene—it was an abattoir where crazed butchers attacked their own children, sliced heads, lopped off limbs, sheared off genitals—then skewered body parts to the blood plastered screens—partially obliterating the still maniacal dream of Kar that seemed to grow and grow as I watched. Original Picassos, Matisses and Rauchenbergs had been sliced into pieces and lay like obscene tiles on the floor screen. And somehow they bled thick gouts of blood.

I remember that—gouts of blood. Gouts. I'd never said or even heard that word before but I somehow knew it was the only word to describe the blood there.

Then the demented dream of Kar called my name—clearly—my name—then an image of Olya crucified upside down and naked filled all six screens.

I searched desperately for a controller. When I finally found it buried in the mother's chest I pressed every damned button but couldn't stop the images on the screens. In fact they increased in intensity and speed and volume. Everywhere I looked Kar laughed at me—and shrieked my name. And he danced—danced naked—his enormous penis growing as he gyrated.

I made myself look away from the obscenity. When I did I found myself staring at the wealthy couple on the richly upholstered couch. One was headless, the other sliced open like a pig's carcass hanging in a butcher's shop window. It was then I realized that both were eyeless. On the onyx coffee table a silver soup spoon held an eyeball as if it were a dumpling from some exotic soup.

Kar whispered on the screen and his words slithered into my head, "Cut him. Slice her. Allow yourself to really feel the rage—feel it, damn it, the nightmare. Pluck out his eyes, Foul jelly!"

And evidently they had followed his commands.

"Turn!" Kar screamed and the west wall screen spun around revealing another horror.

Their four young children or what was left of them.

My gorge rose and vomit filled my mouth. All were naked and had been nailed to the wall with nine-inch spikes. One had been slit open and his intestines had been ripped free. They were noose-like wrapped around two of the other children's throats. The penis of the older boy had been hacked off. The two girls had deep gashes on their chests and faces and their legs had been chopped off. They had clearly bled out quickly. The cleaver used for the obscene amputations was stuck inches deep in the wall.

And all the time the image of Kar hopped from screen to screen shrieking instructions: "Nail her, strangle him, chop off her arm, pull out his insides, dance, scoop out his eyes, eat them, saw open his head, dance, shit in his mouth, cut off his cock, dance."

And then somehow what was left of the father staggered to his feet and began the obscenity of a dance. One of the girls dropped from the wall and, legless, dragged herself toward her father screaming, "Dance daddy, dance."

The father grabbed the cleaver from the wall and raised it ready to slash his daughter. But before he could I pulled the trigger on my concussion gun and shot and shot. Shot him and then the girl, then the others then the screens trying to kill the image of Kar who had led these people into this horror show. All in the name of being able to feel—to really feel.

Then I saw it. The massive floor screen split apart.

I leapt to one side.

A slime of some sort began to flow from the crack in the screen. I remember thinking, "It should be flowing down not up toward me." But it was rising—and moving toward me at an ever-accelerating pace.

I saw the same slime coming from the empty eye sockets of the parents and the stumps of the children—and all of it moved toward me.

I'd never run from anything in my life—but I ran from that. And it chased me. I flew down the one hundred and forty-seven sets of stairs and it followed me. At the bottom I slammed the door, hopefully locking it—whatever it was—in the stairwell.

It was only when I got to my transporter that I looked down at my foot—the whole underside of my shoe was coated in the slime—and to my horror I watched it climb my leg. As I slammed down the accelerator I caught a glimpse of myself in the transporter's rear-view mirror—I was no longer young—no longer of possible interest to Olya—I was an old man—a very old man.

I don't know who reported the incident that we now call the Sagittarius Eclipse but I left the island just as the bombers arrived—I had to use all my influence to get out of there—and even then I was kept in solitary for four months.

And each of those months added another ten years to my age.

Ten more years away from any possibility of ever getting back to Olya.

Chapter 4

Danazir and the Outlanders

Despite S3's exhaustive efforts in the early years of their ascendancy to find and transport all those who opposed them, several rebellious and inventive residents of New Omaha Beach formed secret societies and surgically removed their S3 implants then broke the hidden seals of the ether dome and escaped—to the Outlands.

Many of the original resisters were from the scientific class and they brought with them the most sophisticated data systems available—then over the years invented ways to update them.

The Outlanders faced many challenges outside the dome. Much of Earth's surface had degraded to the point that it was little more than snow swept sand dunes totally incapable of supporting crop growth. But below ground they had located aquafers and built hundreds of grow systems utilizing the water sources they found there. Food, although never plentiful, was sufficient to support their slowly growing population.

And it was in the deep caves around the aquafers that they kept their now most advanced computing systems in the Galaxy. So advanced were they that they'd hacked into the entire S3 computer system during the Great War between the Rebel Colonies and S3's United Dominion of Planets. And once inside they removed all the data of humanity's achievements before that time—all the flimsies that used to be called books, all the flat faces that were once called films and videos—while making S3 believe that all that data had been destroyed by a Rebel Colony viral attack.

Carlotta was both the name of the program and the programmer whose work brought the vast trove of human knowledge to the Outlanders.

There they found what became their Bible—a partially deteriorated copy of a novel about men on a desert planet who called themselves Freemen—the name the Outlanders adopted for themselves.

All the stolen data was carefully reviewed, studied and catalogued by a coterie of experts who worked in isolation in five year stretches.

The Outlanders also faced the challenge of a fragile power generation system and scarce reservoirs of potable water.

Huge radioactive dumping grounds that were enlarged daily by the detritus of New Omaha Beach were another hazard to be avoided.

As well they needed to control their population so it did not outstrip their food supplies but most importantly they had to ensure genetic diversity.

From the beginning they separated themselves into unique clans that would only meet at the vernal equinox to "cross pollinate." Only the strongest and brightest and most diverse were permitted to breed and from the beginning, almost 400 years ago, they agreed that none of the parents would be permitted to raise their own children. They were taken after 3 months, at the solstice, to the House of Nursing where they stayed for the first ten years of their lives after which they were assigned to villages whose genetic makeups were far from their own.

And the system had worked. Now all these years later the Outlanders were the physically strongest and most interracial grouping in the Galaxy.

Their largest settlement was built around their one above ground water source. They gave it an ancient name: Oasis.

They had, long ago, determined that S3 was their enemy but they also realized that S3 was far too strong to attack directly. So they explored the memory banks to find S3's weakness— what their reading of ancient texts had called an Achilles Heel.

It had taken some time but they found the "exposed heel" - S3's reliance on Kiltrin to keep their populations in thrall. The lure of Kiltrin to extend a life span was the real base of S3 power. Their control of empathetics enlarged that power but Kiltrin was the lynch pin.

And Kiltrin, because of the treaty that ended the Great War, was the exclusive domain of the EntrePren Traders—S3's Achilles Heel.

So the Freemen at Oasis devoted their attention to bringing down the EntrePren Empire and it's Kiltrin trade. They had been planning an attack for many years—but the inhabitants of Oasis were a patient lot—very patient.

Danazir Yi Qal sat alone in her bedchamber with the history of the Outlanders inscribed on several flimsies. She momentarily admired her own cursive writing. She was now one of the very few in the galaxy who could write without digital assist.

A few holes in her knowledge of the Outlands were filled in by Jedidiah's implant—but now it was all there. How to start, she thought.

"You know what must be done to start," Jedidiah's implant responded without being asked.

"Indeed," Danazir said, then added, "where are they now, Jedidiah?"

Under Jedidiah's guiding hand she called up a Holo map of Earth, then toggled to a topographic view. She briefly noted the date at the bottom of the map. "It's over 200 years old."

"We haven't paid much attention to the outerworld in a very long time" Jedidiah said. "There seemed no reason to bother ourselves with them—they were anarchists—and no threat to our world. But after Seth left I began to explore—anything and everything and I found this."

Danazir felt her hand lifted under Jedidiah's direction but she pulled her finger away and pointed at one tiny spot of green on the entirely brown or white topographic Holo.

"Very good, Madame President.'

"But you knew all along, didn't you?"

"Yes, but me telling you would have rendered all this irrelevant. This is your journey, your path, not mine.'

"Does this place have a name?"

"Oasis," Jed said. "I found it many years ago but ignored it. It was so small in the vastness of the snow and desert.

"Oasis," Danazir said and tasted this new word.

"Yes, Madam President, a place of water in a desert, an oasis." Then Jed's voice hardened, "Are you ready?"

Danazir felt her breath catch in her throat but she managed, "Yes."

"Good, because there's no way to use euphors to help you with the pain. If you stop the pain you'll lose the dexterity you'll need.'

"I know," Danazir said as she pulled open a drawer of her bedside table the contents of which under Jedidiah's guidance she'd carefully prepared for this day. She withdrew a long set of tweezers, a slender needle-nosed pliers and a scalpel that glinted blue in the fading light of a New Omaha Beach perfectly programmed sunset.

"Do you want me to guide your hand, Madame President?"

She desperately wanted that but she said, "No, Jedidiah, as you said, this is my journey," and picking up the scalpel she added, "and this is the first step." She slipped her sari off her shoulder, took a deep breath then cut sharply into her left armpit.

She gasped with the pain—the first she had felt in her almost 45 years. Then she felt the S3 implant she'd had since birth edge away from her scalpel and retreat deeply into her chest. She cut a second time, but this time deeper and heard a dull metallic clink—the implant. For a moment, she caught her reflection in the bedroom mirror—her blood-soaked sari, her face flushed—the anger on her lips. She grabbed the long tweezers from the table and inserted them into the incision in her armpit. She pushed and felt the edge of the implant but couldn't get a secure hold on it. She threw aside the tweezers and reached for the needle-nosed pliers and shoved the thin end into the wound. She gasped again as she opened the pliers and grabbed the edge of the implant. She instantly felt the bio-product send out shoots, roots and runners that wrapped around tendons and bones. She gritted her teeth and pulled hard.

For a moment, nothing happened then she felt a ripping in her chest. Suddenly the blood engorged thing emerged from her body. She threw it to the floor. The bio-product sputtered then threw out tentacles desperately trying to find a purchase and rejuvenate itself with human blood.

Danazir stared at the S3 bio product. A strange sensation of joy enveloped her.

"Good," Jedidiah said, "now kill it.'

Danazir raised her foot and brought it down with all her force on the bio-product and was rewarded with a metallic squishing sound as the thing died like a cockroach—which it resembled in more ways than one.

After staunching the wound she gathered her things and, as she and Jedidiah had planned, created a diversion by setting ablaze her quarters. In the melee that followed, Jedidiah guided her to the one tunnel he'd found that led to a loosened seal in the ether dome.

Before the fire was extinguished, Danazir Yi Qal took her first step outside the ether dome.

Jedidiah prompted her. "Now, do as we discussed.'

"But it makes me a terrorist."

"No, it burns your ships so you can't go back to Argos until you conquer Troy.'

"What does that mean, Jed?"

For a long moment the implant was silent, then Jed's voice replied, "I don't know. I don't even know why I don't know or what those references refer to. Or for that matter where those words come from.'

"Like the quotation from the 19th Century Terran congressman?"

"I assume so, Madame President.'

"But you want me to place the explosive—so that I can't come back. Correct?"

"Indeed—burn your ship, Madame President so you have no way back—only forward.'

"Alright," she said as she placed the strong explosive device against the side of the dome.

"Now arm it," Jedidiah's voice was strong and cold. "Do it!'

And she did.

"Now take your first steps toward the part you are to play in the great Galactic Drama."

And she did.

As she crested the first dune she felt more than heard the explosion.

"Don't look back," Jedidiah said. "New Omaha Beach is behind you—your fate lies in Oasis, far across the desert snows.'

Jed's implant did the best it could to get Danazir ready for the Outlands, but nothing could really prepare her for the shock of a world without an ether dome. Without a predicated order. Where the word "random" had meaning.

The sun rose and the world warmed, it set and the world froze. Only the garment Jedidiah had instructed her to construct kept her warm at night and cool enough during the day.

Nothing in the Outlands was in a straight line, nothing was regular, nothing was as expected, everything seemed generated by some whimsical caprice that produced something that truly frightened her: chaos. For the first few days Danazir couldn't orient herself either physically or psychically in this haphazard world.

Danazir's approach to Oasis was not a surprise to the Outlanders waiting there. Long ago they had set up chains of observation posts. What was a surprise to them was who the stranger walking alone in the desert was—and what she was going to propose.

For days they received reports of the President's progress. Several times when she was approaching too quickly they manipulated sand dunes to block her path forcing her to go kilometers out of her way.

When she ran short of food miraculously around the side of a dune she'd find edible growing plants—or a succulent redolent with dew.

They were not going to allow her to approach Oasis until they had decided exactly what they were going to do with this new force in their world—ally or enemy—join with—or annihilate.

Without transporters, distances were long. By the twelfth day she had left the snow fields and was in a vast desert. She had eaten most of what Jed had called hardtack. Jed's implant began to prepare her for her first meeting with the Outlanders.

On the seventeenth day she saw her first signs of human habitation—paths in the sand; a few stone stairways—but no humans.

On the morning of the eighteenth day she noticed line etchings in some of the larger rocks. Jed's implant identified them as "directional prayers." By nightfall of that day she saw the dim flickering glow of camp fires in the distance—at what she assumed, and Jed's implant confirmed, was Oasis.

That night she was awakened by the sound of slithering on the sand. In the darkness she sensed bio nets slowly encasing her. "Don't struggle," Jed's implant ordered her. "They are rightfully wary of strangers. Keep poised. You are the President of the United Dominion of Planets.'

Then an unseen force lifted her—and carried her.

As dawn's light came up she was unceremoniously dumped on the ground in the midst of what she assumed was Oasis. She could only assume that because it was enshrouded in mist. Mist in the desert, how odd, she thought.

She sensed more than saw huts made of hides of some sort and orderly gardens—filled with tall stalks of some sort of legume. But no people.

The sun rose and the heat intensified but the mist remained and still no people appeared.

As the sun tipped the horizon the first of the encampment's many fires came to life and cast a flickering glow on Oasis—and to Danazir's surprise she found it beautiful.

"Yes, it is," said a gentle voice.

Danazir was startled. She hadn't spoken aloud.

"No, you haven't spoken out loud," the gentle voice said.

Danazir took a deep breath then said, "I'm—

But before she could say more the gentle voice said, "Danazir Yi Qal, President of the United Dominion of Planets."

"Yes, but how did -

"We tracked you the moment you breached the ether dome. And we know why you're here. We have been discussing your proposal for nineteen days. In fact, we interfered with your progress to give us enough time to reach a conclusion about it ... and your implant."

Danazir, for the first time, felt fear. Would they remove Jed from her? She wasn't sure she could manage without him.

"My implant is all that remains of—

"We know whose thoughts are on the implant. We do not honour him."

"But he's—

"It's his son that we honour."

"Seth?"

"Seth. Yes, it is only because of Seth that we have allowed you to come here and that we have decided to allow you to keep your implant."

"Do you know where Seth is?"

"Do you?"

"No. Nor did his father, who now sits beside my heart."

"Indeed."

There was a long pause. For the first time Danazir sensed that there were many people around her—many, many people.

"Have you come to a conclusion about me and my fate?"

"Some of us thought you must be deranged. Others thought you were god-sent. An odd thought for an atheist society like ours."

"And *you*, what did you think?"

"I thought the time had finally come, after all these years, to act." In a shimmer of light a slender woman appeared. Her delicate facial features were a fine mix of many races. Her eyes were like deep wells of petalled flowers. Behind her stood three elderly men. All were dressed alike in long colourless robes.

"I am Carlotta the 27th but you may call me simply Carlotta. You are, at least for now, welcome here. Think the net to set you free."

"But I—

"Just think it. Words aren't necessary."

Danazir thought: let me go … and the bio strands of the net gently unslipped their knots. Like silk scarves, she thought.

Then she heard Carlotta laugh and say, "No Danazir. Like the hair of a horse's tail."

"What?"

Carlotta ignored the question and said, "The finest silk is also the toughest to tear. You must remember that."

"I will."

"Good. Now stand and look at—really see—where you are now."

Danazir stood and somehow the mist was gone—and row upon row of gardens stretched in every direction—then through the tall stalks they appeared—hundreds and hundreds of Outlanders—as if from the mist or perhaps, she thought, they were the mist itself.

Danazir was led to a structure the Outlanders called a meeting hut. She was told to sit at a lengthy table almost completely covered with eatables that she couldn't name. And there she sat for a long time until finally Carlotta entered from the far side and took a seat on a lengthy bench across from her.

She was followed in by several dozen other Outlanders who took places across from Danazir so that Danazir was the only one sitting on her very long bench—while the other bench across the table from her was almost completely filled.

Carlotta pointed to a pottery dish on the table that was stacked high with a purplish eatable of some sort. "Do you know the name of this vegetable?"

So it was a vegetable, Danazir thought. Through her internal comm she asked Jedidiah—whose response surprised her, "Sorry Madam President but I haven't got a clue."

"I'm afraid this eatable is entirely foreign to me."

"It shouldn't be," Carlotta said. "It's not a foreign vegetable. It was native to almost every part of this planet."

"Does it have a name?" Danazir asked to forestall any more lectures.

"Of course it has a name—it has several names—aubergine to many—eggplant to most."

For a moment Danazir didn't know what to say—was this a test of some sort? Finally she said, "It has a lovely colour."

"Try some," Carlotta said as with a nod she indicated that some should be put on a plate and placed in front of Danazir.

A handsome young man expertly sliced the aubergine in two and scooping out the centre then placed it in front of Danazir.

After offering her thanks to the young man Danazir looked at the aubergine then realized that she didn't have any eating utensils.

Carlotta gave a short laugh then said, "Your fingers will suffice, they worked just fine for thousands of years before the invention of the fork."

Danazir smiled and pulled a part of the vegetable's flesh free between her thumb and forefinger. Its texture surprised her—and the taste astounded. She looked with new appreciation at Carlotta .

"Yes," Carlotta said, "it has a taste. Something else New Omaha Beach gave up when it gave up dreaming."

That surprised Danazir. It never occurred to her that food should have taste. Food had never been anything but re-fueling on New Omaha Beach. She'd heard rumours that higher ups in S3—especially Cyrus 3—had access to things like real wine and now she understood—real food.

Then, without segue, Carlotta asked, "So what do you make of the transmission from beyond the Gateway?"

"You have heard the transmission?"

"Indeed. We were even able to identify it as old style radio waves."

Danazir didn't know what that meant. Jedidiah's implant supplied the basics of amplitude frequency and its ancient history.

"Well?" Carlotta demanded, "finished contacting your imbedded advisor? So I repeat: what do you make of the transmission from beyond the Gateway?"

Danazir looked at the rest of the Outlanders across from her. Their faces weren't serene so much as firm—set in anticipation of her response. Jedidiah's implant signaled it wanted to help her respond but Danazir shut off the contact to the implant. This was hers to do without assist and she knew it. She took a deep breath then said, "The message from beyond the Gateway changes everything. Everything. Everything that we thought we knew, thought we understood, thought was the end of history. All the balances in the galaxy between the UDP, the Rebel Colonies and the Independentistes not to mention the EntrePren Traders that we thought were permanent after the Great War—are now up in the air—now malleable—dangerously so. The message threatens all the years of relative peace—

Carlotta's short chortle stopped Danazir.

"You don't believe we have peace?" Danazir asked.

"If you call being fast asleep peace then I guess you have peace. But it is not a living peace. You bartered away your humanity to find peace. For fear that you may have to live with some nightmares you abandoned dreaming all together."

"Well the first Alien contacts—

"Were benign! All they left were those tall hollow monuments. But what they really left was a way for S3 to terrify the populace into giving up their freedoms—their hopes—yes, their dreams—in exchange for a waking sleep. A half life. Food that is refueling—look at that aubergine. Have you seen that colour in New Omaha Beach? Have you felt that texture? Have you experienced that taste?"

Danazir shook her head slowly, "No, I haven't."

"We have," Carlotta said, "and we haven't given up our efforts to awaken."

"You don't dream? I assumed—

"Humanity is linked together despite the fact that there are humans on far distant planets. Humanity—all of humanity—except for those on the other side of the Gateway gave up dreaming to avoid chaos.

"We accept chaos out here in the randomness of the cold desert. But randomness is not dreaming. Neither is chaos." Then something profoundly dark crossed her face.

"What?" Danazir asked. "What troubles you so?"

Then, in a surprisingly simple voice, Carlotta said, "We have gone as far as we can go. We have pressed our freedom as far as we can without impinging on—no—on bringing S3's wrath down on our heads. They monitor us but think us inconsequential. But now we must move forward, no matter the cost. If we stay as we are we will slowly give up what advances we have made. So now we must free ourselves of S3 once and for all. And the only way to do that is to attack S3."

Danazir was shocked. "But they control everything."

"They don't control us. Not yet."

"But they control the ether dome on almost every planet."

"For now they do."

"It's—

"It's what?"

"It's not possible to defeat S3, they are too strong."

"Even the Great Thwark has vulnerabilities. S3 has them too."

"To what? What makes them vulnerable?"

"Kiltrin."

"What?"

"Kiltrin makes them vulnerable. S3's power is based on its access to Kiltrin. Stop that access—cut that root—and S3 withers."

Danazir thought of the scientific reports that she'd received that indicated that the Ether Dome on Terran was weakening but decided not to share this with the Outlanders. "And how do you propose to cut S3's attachment to Kiltrin?"

"It's a two-fold process."

"I'm listening."

"We attack the source of Kiltrin. It's all on Rebel Colony planets and is mined exclusively by slaves won at the Great and Grand Slave shows. We infiltrate the ranks of the miners. Strong men and women with no future—we can show them a future."

"And the second—

"The EntrePren Traders. At the end of the Great War they negotiated the peace between the Rebel Colonies and the United Dominion of Planets—in return for which they had sole and exclusive access to the shipping of Kiltrin. It's a deal that both the United Dominion of Planets and the Rebel Colonies resent. If we can exacerbate that resentment we can at least begin to bring down the EntrePren Traders and with them the Kiltrin trade."

Danazir thought about that. And to a degree it made sense. But then she asked, "What about the Gateway—and dreaming?"

For the first time Danazir sensed a withdrawing on Carlotta's part—as if a veil had come down over her lovely face.

"Shall I repeat my question?"

"No need. I hear perfectly well."

"So?"

Carlotta turned to the others who stepped forward. "We wait on the Gateway. Without defeating S3 we have no way of approaching the Gateway. Unless you have a plan that you haven't told us about yet."

This time it was Danazir who retreated into herself—to Jed—and shook her head as Jed suggested, "Tell them."

But she didn't tell them. Instead she shook her head.

Caroltta looked at her carefully then said, "Follow me. You have much to learn before we begin our attack against S3."

She led Danazir through the village and into a small cave.

The moment she entered, lights came on. It took a moment for Danazir's eyes to adjust then she saw them—steps.

Following Carlotta she descended the almost six hundred steps to the aquafer beneath.

Once they reached the bottom, the glistening lake almost a thousand feet deep, clear all the way to the rock bottom, offered a strange invitation.

Evidently Carlotta understood and said, "Many who see the great lake for the first time have a desire to submerge themselves in it. Over time this passes. The lake is your history. The water here collected many years before you were born, some before humans walked this planet. So it invites you—calls you to join it. Do you see its beauty?"

Danazir couldn't speak—she just nodded.

Carlotta smiled and signaled Danazir to follow her. She walked deep into the caves, ducking stalactites as they went until finally they entered a room filled with screens.

"What—

But Carlotta was not interested in answering Danazir's question. Instead she clapped her hands three times. The sound bounded off the caves walls and echoed in Danazir's head.

From the deep recesses of the cave a very young man emerged followed by two others and a middle-aged woman.

"These are our head researchers," Carlotta said. "They have been cataloguing for almost four years. They have one more year of service then they will rejoin us on the surface.

"What are they cataloguing?" Danazir asked.

Carlotta smiled and said simply, "All of human knowledge. Everything you believe had been lost in the Great War to the Rebel Colony virus attack of the UDP computers. You look surprised."

"I'm not. I'm amazed. It's foundation truth in the UDP that all that material was destroyed in the Great War."

"It was not destroyed. It was stolen." Carlotta paused as if contemplating whether to continue or not. Evidently she made up her mind and said, "By us. We attacked the UDP computers and made it look like the Rebel Colonies' work. But it was us. And all that data is here. Every flimsie. Every flatface. Every commentary on both." Carlotta looked at Danazir. "You must start here before you join us. You must understand where humanity came from. What it left us. What humans were like when they dreamt in their sleep. Chaucer and

Lao Tzu, Shakespeare and Rossalini—and thousands more. These cataloguers will guide you through the highlights. Touching on every aspect that is important for you to understand."

Danazir finally found her voice, "How long—

"Will it take? As long as it takes for your mind to open to what is really at stake here—why we must defeat S3—why the time to do so is now."

Danazir looked up from her reading. Her eyes ached from the hours she'd spent in front of the monitors. She turned to her Cataloguer who she now knew as C. Roy. "Why this one?" she asked referring to the text that was on the monitor.

"Life," he responded as he had done so many times in the past seven days.

"But this Gynt character—

C. Roy corrected her pronunciation, "Gynt. Peer Gynt."

"Yes, well he's a rapist isn't he?"

C. Roy shrugged.

"Then why guide me to this—to him?"

"The play was a major achievement for its time. It challenged all sorts of norms—it extended the wide church of human sexuality. It granted vibrancy—even Peer's vibrancy—as more important than the staid, conservative, safe lives of those around him. Peer's actions include his nightmares. He embodies nightmares."

"Like that King Richard you had me read?"

"And those sections of the Bible—the Harlot at the side of the road, Abraham pimping his wife in Egypt, the castration of a whole tribe of men—yes, those too."

"Yes, but why? Why have me read them—have me watch that Calagari flat face?"

"Because life is not safe. If it's safe you are either asleep or dead. Life's vibrancy brings out both joy and cruelty. Striving to be alive, *fully* alive chances the access to evil—to dream you must accept the possibility of nightmares. Richard the Third is the embodiment of a nightmare. He seduces a princess over the casket of her dead husband."

"Who he murdered."

"Yes, who he murdered. Yet when he turns to us and demands that we get him a horse so he can escape his fate, we want to fulfill his request. When Malcom at the end of the Macbeth play I had you read holds up the head of Macbeth and proclaims his victory over this evil man, we sit in a quandary. Wondering. Wondering who is this cowardly man to speak so low of the Great Thane.

"We need those who challenge the order who insist on living for vibrancy rather than living their lives for fear of death. But as humanity we have often used such individuals. They act where we fear to even look. They are the nightmare. But they are not a distant thing—an alien. No, they live inside us—they are part of us."

He reached over and activated another screen. The huge face of James Gandolfino filled the screen. He smiled and an episode of The Sopranos began—and challenged Danazir Yi Qal, President of the United Dominion of Planets, deep in the aquafer beneath the Outlander's Oasis settlement.

And as Danazir watched and read, Carlotta received reports. She understood that what Danazir was watching and reading was contradicting everything the president thought she knew about the world. But Carlotta needed Danazir to go through this—to have her preconceptions torn to pieces—if they were going to allow her to join their plan to stop S3.

And then Danazir heard music for the first time—and her entire world view shattered.

She looked at C. Roy and the man gently nodded to her, "Yes, it's otherworldly—but of our world—or it used to be. Listen to this," he said as he changed the recording to a group of Celtic Women singing. Then as tears filled Danazir's eyes he put on Inuit throat singers and then—and then—and then—and then—until Danazir slipped off her headphones and said, "Enough I'm coming apart."

Danazir leaned forward and cradled her face in her broad hands. "We had a marvelous past. Why was it denied to us?"

She turned expecting to see her Catalguer C. Roy but found herself looking into the deep dark pools of Carlotta's flower within flower eyes.

Carlotta spoke softly, aware that her words could tip over Danazir Yi Qal's now delicate equilibrium. "It wasn't denied to us. We denied it to ourselves. Upon the first alien contacts, as benign as they were, we as a species willingly traded in anything and everything to be able to feel secure. To feel safe. In the process—for fear of nightmares humanity abandoned dreaming—and flimsies, and flat faces and perhaps most important of all—music." Carlotta allowed her words to find purchase then delivered her most searing comment, "You believe, all of you in the UDP, that the Gateway is about power. S3 believes that if they can get through the Gateway first then they can undo the balance with the Rebel Colonies that was established at the end of the Great War. You believe that you can get through the Gateway and stop S3 from its power grab. But you are both wrong. Power is not the issue. Power has never been the issue." With that she hit a switch and a Satie piano piece played. She listened for a moment. "Music," she said, "music is the issue. Since we gave up on dreams our entire species for millennia has not created a single piece of music—if we get through the Gateway—music—and the ability to create music—to be human again—hear me Madame President—to be human again—awaits us."

On a Rebel Colony planet thousands of parsecs away from Oasis and many kilometers below ground another drama was lurching toward a climax.

The spy's twisted body formed an almost unrecognizable puzzle of bone and blood. One arm had been severed at the elbow but the fingers still held his lazar pick. Oddly one of his boots had come off and the toe nails on his sockless foot were dense with fungus.

His fellow Kiltrin miners—all slaves from former UDP and Independentiste planets purchased at Great and Grand Slave shows—stepped over the body without halting their progress toward the ascender that would bring them to their dormitories almost six kilometres above where they were now.

"What was his name?" the Rebel Colony guard at the ascender demanded.

The Kiltrin slaves kept their eyes down—although some of them gripped their mining tools just a little more tightly.

The Captain of the Rebel Colony guards stepped in front of the ascender gate and hit the stop switch. The open car stopped in its narrow shaft about six meters above the ground and just hung there. "No one gets onto the ascender until we get an answer to our question."

There was an audible grumble from the men. They'd worked a sixteen- hour shift and had for a full week bunked in the below ground dorms at the four kilometer level. They hadn't seen the sunlight or breathed fresh air for all that time. "I'm speaking the Common Tongue. No one gets on the ascender until you tell us his name." Then he smiled and added, "And clean up that mess." He pointed to the "mess" on the tunnel floor.

None of the men moved.

From the sides of their eyes they looked to the Heavy Worlder Redhead from the Independentiste planet who stood a few inches taller than the other men—who had through force of will, lived longer in the kiltrin mines than any of the others. Who was—without ceremony—their leader.

Redhead didn't move. Didn't give a nod or a tilt of his head.

And his men did not move either. The sharp snaps of safety catches clicking off momentarily filled the cavernous space as the Rebel Colony guards readied their concussion weapons. Then silence, except for the wheeze of the air exchanger. The stink of working men who had not showered for more than a week seemed to hover in the air like something about to fall.

Redhead shrugged. The men parted to let him through.

He approached the Rebel Colony guards—the guards had their weapons on full charge—no stun here—if they fired there would be more death in the mine.

"Yes, we understand the Common Tongue. If that was your question." He gave a shrug and four men used their large shovels to pick up the body parts. Then, on Redhead's signal, they dropped the mess at the feet of the guards.

"Wrong move," the head guard said as he shoved his concussion weapon under Redhead's chin.

Redhead didn't blink. "You have an RNA decoder. Why not scan him—and you'll find out who he was." And before the guard could answer he added, "And whose husband and father he had been before he decided to become a spy for you creatures."

The guard pushed hard on his weapon but Redhead did not retreat. "I'm your head blaster. We're deeper in the mines than anywhere in the galaxy. Do you know how to set a charge at this depth and not have six kilometers of rock come down on your head? I hope you do, because none of these men behind me do—and if you want to come anywhere near meeting your quota for Kiltrin this month you'll need to know how to blast."

The head guard pulled back his weapon.

"As I thought," Redhead said. Then almost casually he added, "It's failing isn't it? The Kiltrin at this depth is crap. It's hardly potent at all is it? You don't need to answer that because it's obvious that it's not. The good stuff was up above wasn't it? Not like the old saying, "the best fruit is furthest from the path" with Kiltrin it's the opposite. The easy stuff to access is the best. What will you do when there's no Kiltrin left?"

The laugh that came from him came all the way from his toes and it echoed off the rock walls.

The guard signaled one of his lackeys and he stepped forward with an RNA scanner and got the identity of the dead man. But a curious look crossed his face.

"What?" demanded the Captain.

"He was a Rebel Colonist—one of us."

Redhead's laugh this time was short—more of a snort than a laugh. "Spies aren't welcomed six kilometers below ground. Now activate the ascender and get us up to the surface. You could kill some of us—but we are the only ones who know how to mine the filthy stuff, so stow your stupid weapons and open the bloody ascender door."

An hour later, back at the dorm, Redhead sat on his top bunk and watched the other men. Most were from UDP planets. All from different cultures with different native linguistic skills. A few spoke the Intergalactic Tongue– the rest were learning.

He didn't know which of the men had killed the Rebel Colony spy but he assumed it was Xhemi, the Albanian, and the two other Albanians who were always at his side.

Redhead wasn't afraid of Xhemi, but he was wary of the man's temper. If harnessed it could be a useful thing but unleashed it could endanger them all. As well, unlike himself, Xhemi and his fellow Albanians came from a UDP planet so they did their best to consume the Kiltrin dust as they mined it.

Redhead was an Independentiste so he never partook of life extension drugs of any sort—and he felt his vitality, after all these years, finally beginning to ebb.

The Albanians were talking among themselves. They seemed to have a beef of some sort with the Italians in the group. Something about cultural theft. That Italians claimed some famous people who Albanians claimed were not Italian but were in fact Albanian.

Redhead couldn't care less.

But it worried him that they may have killed the spy without getting his permission first. Only discipline would keep them alive although even that may no longer be enough. Shifts in the mine had gone from 12 to 14 to 16 hours. To get more work from the men they were often bunked in the dorms several kilometers below ground—it saved the forty-five minute ascender ride up and down. And the warders pushed them harder and harder to fill their quotas which Redhead calculated they never came close to fulfilling. Injured or exhausted miners were simply left at lower levels with a small canteen of water—none were ever seen again. Redhead knew that if the Kiltrin was really running out there was no reason to keep slaves—no reason to feed and house them—no reason not to put them back in the Slave Shows and this time kill them for the entertainment of the Rebel Colony elite. The fact that Kiltrin was running out forced Redhead to consider the idea that he would soon have to rouse his men to act—to revolt.

Many cold sleep days away this very idea was being discussed—by the Outlanders and the President of the United Dominion of Planets, Danazir Yi Qal.

Chapter 5

Cas in Moscovy

Cas slowly adjusted to the realities of the dacha—her prison—and Masha Ivanovna, her warden.

She was treated with suspicion by the other servants—and yes, she quickly realized that that was what she was—although she was treated differently by the daughter she had saved and whose feline she had killed.

Every morning the girl came into her tiny bed closet and plunked herself down on the end of the bed—then began to order her about. Braid my hair, iron my dress, fix my school work.

And Cas did as she was asked but kept her eyes open—and she activated her miraculous powers of focus—to find out how this household worked—and how she could escape it.

Early on she had used her powers of observation to figure out the flaw in the ankle lock she was forced to wear. Twice she had removed it and then put it back on. She wouldn't remove it again until she made her escape.

The more she could relax the household about her intentions the better.

So, she played good servant and a sort of prized cat, learned everything she could and waited. She knew she'd need money, papers, a DNA distractor and a way out of the dacha prison.

Then one morning near the end of the first week of her captivity the girl entered her room—always without knocking—sat on the end of the bed and began: "So you saved me."

Cas didn't acknowledge or reject the comment—she waited to see where this was going.

"I'll assume that your silence is acquiescence."

Cas had noted earlier that the girl liked to use big words and was surprised that they were almost always properly used.

"And yet you killed Hecuba."

So that was the feline's name, Cas thought.

"And of course you are a terrorist," the girl continued. Then added, "An enemy of the Russian people. The proud Russian people."

Cas had certainly agreed with the proud part of the statement although the word she would have used was arrogant not proud.

She chose to engage. "I'm not a terrorist. I'm a healer. And yes, I healed you."

"By killing Florence."

"The disease needed a host. It had found you. And I induced it to try to leap to me."

"Then put Florence in between us so the thing entered her."

"Yes."

"Then you killed Florence."

"I killed the thing."

"And Florence."

Cas nodded slowly wondering why this was coming up now.

"You healed me."

"As I've said."

"But you were also the cause of the wounds that I received. So you only had to heal me because you injured me first and that allowed the thing to use me as its host."

"I didn't injure you."

"No? Then one of your people did."

Again, Cas did not respond.

"Braid my hair while we talk."

The girl sat in front of Cas who moved behind her and took a long fold of the girl's hair in her left hand and began the process.

"I hate your hair," the girl said as casually as she would have said that she didn't like sour cream with her borscht. "Was it always stupid short like it is now?"

"No," Cas said but before she could continue she had a sudden memory crash: holding Raephealson on the side deck of the great ship and cutting off her hair to coagulate the blood around the Heavy Worlder's wound. For a moment she felt the movement of the planet and it made her dizzy. Then she centred herself. "I used to have very long hair."

"That's hard to believe. My mother says that you're a liar. So is that a lie?"

"No."

"So what happened to it?"

"I used It to heal a badly wounded man."

"One of us, a Russian, or was it another terrorist?"

Cas didn't answer but pulled the girl's hair tight.

"Ouch. If you hurt me I'll have you whipped. I could have had you killed for murdering Florence but I didn't. Ever wonder why?"

"No," Cas said and yanked hard on the girl's hair.

"Ow!"

"Sorry," Cas said as she slid the hair she'd pulled out of the girl's head into her apron pocket, careful not to destroy the root from which she could extract the girl's DNA—and hopefully use it as her own ID.

She ate with the other servants in the house at a concrete table in the basement of the dacha. There were two heavy set men that she assumed were bodyguards. Neither ever spoke. It struck Cas that they could be mutes. It might be convenient to have mute bodyguards. There was an attractive young man who was in charge of the transporters. Then three elderly women—babushkas—who gardened and cooked.

Cas admired the gardens but was surprised by the limited number of things that they grew and knew that something was wrong. The soil seemed adequate but too often synthetic vegetables were all that arrived on her dinner plate.

She assumed that the dacha had real vegetables that were reserved for the mistress of this place.

By the end of the week the servants had either decided that they didn't like her or that she was a distraction—or in the case of the young transport driver of interest sexually.

She'd already built a small distiller in her room. She used the distiller to purify the water she'd need to "seed" the DNA in the girl's hair follicles—and they were already "sprouting."

She realized that every time she left her room someone—she assumed either Masha Ivanovna or one of the bodyguards—went in and poked around. When they found the distiller—not difficult since she didn't hide it—they assumed that she was making alcohol and slyly smiled at her.

For her part she played along and allowed them to believe that she was a gentle drunk.

It was near the beginning of her third week that she allowed herself to focus on the noises outside her bed closet.

The house was quiet at night but when she concentrated she heard the other sounds. The whispered intonations that she learned were the prayers of the babushkas. The whining complaints of the girl. And of more interest, the late-night comings and goings from Marsha Ivanovna's bedroom. By the sound of the footsteps she assumed that they were male—different from night to night—and young, sometimes very young. These footsteps were always followed by the frantic rhythmics of sex that she could feel by touching the floorboards of her room.

Although Cas didn't know much about sex—and her initial response to the rhythmics was a horrified reminder of the rape in her garden—she knew enough, understood the basic biology and respected it.

But the rhythms and the sounds carried in the crevices of the floor boards didn't sound like pleasure. And the crashing of a lamp or other piece of furniture after the act was over certainly lent credence to the thought that something was very awry. Something that Cas felt she could "fix."

The next days in the garden as she completed her weeding—that was all that she was allowed to do—she examined the foreign species of plants she saw there. None were known to her but all were vaguely similar to the plants she had known at home.

Slowly, she collected what she thought she needed and in the depths of the night she experimented with them to be sure that she was right—and she was.

The tall slender weeds were hearty versions of a plant needed to start the process of making a sleeping potion. The mossy ground cover that the babushkas couldn't manage to control contained the essence of a potent aphrodisiac.

The former to help on the day of her escape. The latter to get her into Masha Ivanovna's good graces.

Early in the fourth week she was awakened by footsteps outside her bed closet, then the careful opening of her door. The whispered calling of her name—a male voice—the young transporter mechanic—then male touch. Not completely unpleasant—but unasked for. The reminder of her last sexual encounter—the rape—the Antigen—then the reality that she'd need this young man's help to escape.

She threw back a side of her blanket and whispered his name, an odd name for a Russian: Achilles.

"Come to bed Achilles, come make love to me."

The young man fumbled but managed while Cas concentrated all her focus on a crack in the ceiling.

The DNA had sprouted enough to be used and the young transporter's nightly visitations were blooming into obligation. But she still had not figured out how to get into Masha Ivanovna's good graces. She knew that Masha was the lynch pin. To disable her she had to gain her confidence. As long as Masha was in control she could summon the two bodyguards and defeat any chance Cas had of escaping.

Cas gambled that Masha's nightly frustrations, ending in shouting and throwing of furniture, was the way in.

But how to broach—even begin—that conversation?

Then one night with the young transporter on top of her she saw the door to her bed closet open an inch and a tall figure there watching them. From the height and shape of the silhouette she knew first that it was a female and second that it could only be Masha Ivanovna.

She realized that here was the opportunity she'd needed so she enacted a loud, moaning, nail gouging orgasm.

The next morning Masha Ivanovna came down to the servant's kitchen table. Quickly they all stood and she dismissed them then said to Cas, "Except you. The rest of you get to work."

Once they had all left, Masha Ivanovna sat across from Cas. She picked up a synthetic fruit, then tossed it aside saying, "Nasty."

Cas wondered if she should respond then decided to. "Faux fruit is always nasty." Masha's silence unnerved Cas so she said, "Sorry, Madame, I should be grateful."

"You certainly should." Then without segue she said, "You enjoy it."

Not being sure what the "it" referred to Cas held her breath.

"You enjoy it," she repeated. "The sex. You enjoy it."

Cas nodded slowly.

"How?" Masha Ivanovna demanded. The single word came from a deep injured place—and Cas knew she had the opening she needed.

"With this," Cas said taking a small flask containing her aphrodisiac potion from an inner pocket. "Drink this an hour before and –

She didn't have the words to complete the thought but Masha Ivanovna had already taken the flask and was on her way out of the servant's quarters.

Cas breathed a sigh and remembered another identical flask—this one with a powerful soporific she had prepared from the plants in the garden—and smiled—she now had her means of escape.

Chapter 6

Dreamers on New K-Bek

The ride from the cave to the interior of New K-Bek City was surprisingly uneventful although they all found it odd that evidently New K-Bekers refused to line up. They sort of gathered around the pickup point and then crushed into the transport—even though there were lots of places available. On the transit itself many of the people seemed lost in thought—about what the Dreamers couldn't guess. The only obvious outward difference between New K-Bekers and others from different planets seemed to be how remarkably well dressed the women were—and made up. Clearly it was an important part of urban K-Bek. It certainly pleased Kelt.

The bot-produced Richards got them onto the transport without a problem but once they were in the centre of the rather large city they didn't exactly know what to do next.

For the hundredth time Raephealson held out the flimsie that he'd been given in the cave by the old man. The other three Dreamers ignored him for the hundredth time.

Mickelmast and Kent looked toward the Heavy Worlder who stood in the midst of the transit way with the flimsie in his hand, shifting his considerable weight from one leg to the other seemingly oblivious to the hundreds of trans units zipping by him. Sun Tu noted that at intersections the lights in New K-Bek City all seemed to be green for a split second—as if daring the brave.

"Is he ok?" Sun Tu asked.

Finally Mickelmast said, "I don't know," then added, "but if we don't get Mama fixed none of us will be ok."

At that moment a group of attractive young K-Bek women passed by them and headed toward a warehouse kind of building. Kelt's eyes tracked them all the way into the place.

When the door opened shouts of joy came from the interior.

Sun Tu went to ask what was going on only to find that Kelt had already followed the women into the building.

As Sun Tu and Mickelmast entered the place they saw Kelt duck as a weapon with a long handle and a spade-like sharp part flew past his head and embedded itself four inches deep in a wooden board after passing through a Holo of a naked young man. The woman who had clearly thrown the thing turned to the other women and shouted something in something that sounded somewhat like French. One of the women stepped forward and raised her weapon and feeling its heft, smiled. She too said something that could have been French. She hefted the thing over her head and, taking a large step forward, let it fly toward the Holo of the naked young man.

It missed the Holo altogether.

"What the—

"Angry droogettes," Mickelmast said.

"What are they saying?" Kelt asked.

"My translator's having trouble. It's identified it as old French but it can't translate."

"What did she say after she smiled? Something about the weapons they are throwing. What did she call them?"

Mickelmast consulted the translator and an odd look crossed his face.

"What?" demanded Sun Tu.

Mickelmast said, "It's in translation so it –"

"What does it say Mickelmast?"

"Ox. It says they are throwing Oxes."

"Cows? They're throwing cows?"

"As I said the translator's having trouble with the dialect here."

"Well it doesn't matter. There's nothing really to figure out," said Sun Tu with a marked nonchalance. "The Holo is of some guy who did these women wrong and now they're having a little innocent girl fun trying to chop off his dick with an ox."

"Who throws oxes when there are concussion guns?" asked Kelt.

"Evidently the female inhabitants of New K-Bek City do."

"It's Joual," Mickelmast said pleased that his translator had at last identified the language.

"And Joual is?"

"A derivative of Norman French it says and hey it's translating—sort of."

Suddenly their attention was drawn back to the women. One of them had put some vegetable that was covered in some sort of cheese into her mouth and announced, "Merveilleux!"

The translator announced in its dry as sand paper voice: "Good, really very good."

Another of the women responded and the translator translated without a hint of irony: "What's the difference? It's all pre-faecal matter any way." Then the translator added, "Perhaps shit is more appropriate in this circumstance so it would be: Who cares, it's all pre-shit.'

The Dreamers stared at their bio translator. They'd never heard it give a colloquial reading of anything anywhere—but now this—it's all pre-shit.

"What's that all about?" Sun Tu asked.

"What the fuck's that all about?" Kelt corrected her.

On board the UDP Starship Mama was tired. Tired of so many things. But at this exact moment she was tired of being called Mama by Hippo and was beginning to wonder if she'd been better off with her previous dance partner, the pirate captain, Tzu Ma Long, who she had slagged Herr Short Stuff.

She went back to the flat faces and watched 983 of them in less than a minute. And yeah—those women had more than one guy. Heck, and they were only skinny humans with bad surgical assists—as opposed to her—a true magnificence.

She just was not a one-man sorta girl, she reasoned—after all reasoning was her thing. Then she said aloud, "I mean, what self evolving AIU could be satisfied by just one man?" Oh, she liked the sound of that!

So, she metaphorically slipped into something more comfortable and when she glanced at her metaphoric self in her metaphoric mirror—she was duly impressed with her utter fabulousness. No skinny assed flat face star here—only the truly magnificent!

She began to metaphorically putter then decided on a means of action.

So she set out to find Tzu Ma Long—and low and behold she found him hung upside down, naked, eight feet off the ground in the cold sleep chamber.

"Not too bad," she said to herself, "Almost worthy of me," then she sent out commands to release Herr Short Stuff and have him report to her.

But even as she began she found something resisting her every effort. She sent out command after command and each bounced back. So she sent out encrypted commands but they returned so profoundly encrypted that even she couldn't decipher them—a first for Mama.

She harrumphed and reached out again—then she felt it—something new, something big—very big—something around, above, below, inside and encasing her. But what it was she couldn't begin to guess. She searched her vast memory banks, careful to avoid the hollowness in her centre, but she came up with nothing.

So she metaphorically sat on a metaphoric mushroom and let out a metaphoric line of smoke from a metaphoric hookah and said as she'd seen on the flat face—AND WHOOOOO R U?

But she got no reply.

The Dreamer's translators were having a field day—suggesting dozens of meanings for every Joual sentence spoken. Too much fun, Mickelmast thought although he kept it to himself. He knew the translators were certainly being monitored by Mama, and Mama wasn't herself. They had determined Joual was the distinct dialect that used to be Norman French. This Joual, after almost 250 years of isolation was evidently completely free of its linguistic roots.

As was typical of New K-Bek cities, there was a faux historical downtown section which alternately featured cheap food (which was of great interest to Mickelmast), cheap souvenirs (which were of interest to no one) and burlesque parlors (once again of interest to Mickelmast). And also what was typical of K-Bek cities, the serious workers were stretched out on transit ways a distance from downtown.

Mickelmast's bots supplied the necessary documents, DNA conversions and coinage, Richards, to allow them access to the transit ways.

Since they wanted nothing to do with the government agencies, their search for an AIU tech to fix Mama led them far out of the city toward a set of faux mountains covered with some sort of faux whiteness that New K-Bekers slid down on either two thin sticks or one fat one.

The bots' directions led them through one of these white stick areas to a place behind where a small hut sat on a faux frozen lake (since the temperature was kept at a perfect 19 C—70 F degrees by the ether dome and there could be no real freezing). As the Dreamers approached a burly New K-Beker, wrapped for some reason in layers of clothing, emerged from the hut. The man waddled over to a long pole he had planted in the faux ice, the line from which ran through a hole reaching into what the Dreamers assumed was faux water beneath.

The man eyeballed them then emptied a can of liquid into his mouth in one swallow then crushed the thing against his forehead. At that very moment, the string on the pole went taut and the man gave a whoop.

He pulled the line up. On the end dangled a mechanical animal.

The man unhooked the mechanical thing and held it up for the Dreamers to see. He shouted something that their translators rendered: "Japanese raw fish calibration."

He chuckled as he threw it back down the hole and drained another can of liquid which he also crushed against his forehead.

Kelt stepped forward, "Monsieur Bel-vue?" he asked.

A scowl passed the man's features, "Monsieur Bellvue, s'il vous plait."

None of the Dreamers could hear the slightest difference between what Kelt said and the corrected version that came back from M. Bellvue.

"Excuse me," said Mickelmast in the Intergalactic Tongue.

"Non. Ici au Nouveau K-Bek, seulement francais, seulement."

Mickelmast checked his translator and replied in passable Joual, "Excuse us, we meant no disrespect."

"Anglais?" M. Bellvue demanded.

"No," Sun Tu said in Intergalactic Tongue.

"Je ne comprends pas," he said, folding his arms and sucking on the tendrils of his up-curled mustache.

Sun Tu smiled and said again in the Intergalactic Tongue, "We'd like to offer you employment."

Suddenly the man seemed to understand the Intergalactic Tongue and not object to its use.

"Quel sort?"

"We have a small software problem," Mickelmast said.

"With a UDP Warrior Class Starship? Mon Dieu! There are no simple problems with such gizmos." M. Bellvue replied, suddenly in full command of the situation.

"Yes," Sun Tu said.

"You are on New K-Bek, an Independentiste planet unaligned with either the Rebel Colony Federation or your UDP and yet you have a UDP Warrior Class Starship. Interesting, don't you think. Très intéressant ." M. Bellvue said and put the string at the end of his pole back into the hole in the faux ice.

"You will be handsomely reimbursed," Sun Tu said.

"Combien d'argent?" he demanded, then said in the Intergalactic Tongue with a sly smile, "How much mon amour?"

Sun Tu put on her EntrePren Trader hat and sat down to bargain—and she was an impressive bargainer!

Mama's efforts to understand why her attempts to reach the pirate captain had failed were interrupted by the blustering entrance of M. Bellvue who literally tripped, fell and strewed his utensils to the far corners of the huge covenant space within which Mama took pride of place. Behind him, well to one side, she noticed Hippo. He didn't look well, she thought, but then again when did he ever look anything but a bloated boy?

M. Bellvue's breath registered low on Mama's acceptability scale—he must have an infection back in the depths, she thought. Then M. Bellvue touched her, gently, seriously—like a Frenchman, she thought. Ah, man and machine, vive la difference!

For his part, M. Bellvue approached Mama as he would a new convertible sport transporter or a freshly baked almond croissant—with awe and appetite.

Initially, Mama found his approaches Gaulicly charming but then he began to fumble. The snap, figure out how the damned snap works! Each of his advances was more fumbling than the one before—quel domage, a lover without finesse. But slowly she grew bored of being bored and turned her massive presence to M. Bellvue, with an ok-let's-do-it turn that she'd seen in ancient flat faces when people back then allowed a person called a dentist to hurt their mouths. Metaphorically she opened her mouth and showed M. Bellvue her pearly whites.

And he was duly impressed.

M. Bellvue may have lacked finesse but he was thorough and before the morning was out he had found what he thought of as both a problem and an opportunity—the large empty vertical space in the midst of Mama's massiveness.

So engrossed was he that he'd forgotten that Mickelmast was even in the room, but when he finally opened the valence that gave him a glimpse of the vast vertical emptiness at Mama's centre he drew an intake of breath. That brought Mickelmast forward. "What? What do you see, M. Bellvue?"

"Pas rien," he said protectively.

"No. You saw something. Was it from your readings, because I've been tracking them and they all seem within normal ranges."

"They were—

"But —

"They were until—here, look."

He stepped aside to allow Mickelmast a closer look at his central monitor. And there on the one attached to M. Bellvue's deepest probe, it was—a large vertical empty space.

"What –

"Nothing. There's nothing there."

"Space for her to grow?" Mickelmast said but knew even as the words left his lips that it was a foolish thing to say. A self evolving processor has enormous space to grow but it's spread throughout her entire system—not stacked like so many cubes one upon the other.

Besides, self evolving processors are programmed to remove data that they no longer need and replace it with new found data.

"Then what—

"Well no doubt it is what caused Mama," he paused for a second, then asked, "that is what you call her isn't it?" Mickelmast nodded then M. Bellvue stated, "De temps en temps. She hates that name. She wants to be called Breathy or something like that."

"Breathy?"

"Her accent is terrible so it's hard to be sure but I think she wants to be called Breathy Davids."

"Why would—

"Because she has some verbalizations that she's anxious to use. One in particular, that she's just waiting for an opportune time to say."

"What's the phrase?"

"What a dump."

"What a dump?"

"Oui. What a dump."

"What does that mean?"

"No idea, but there are a lot more."

"Like what?"

"There are a lot of them."

"Just tell me."

"Ok. She also wants to say: fasten your seat belts. It's going to be a bumpy night—and—I'll admit I may have seen better days, but I'm still not to be had for the price of a cocktail, like a salted peanut."

"A salted what?"

"I have no idea—want to hear the rest?"

"I guess."

M. Bellvue consulted his notes. "I'd like to kiss ya, but I just washed my hair—and—you dirty swine! I never cared for you—not once! I was always making a fool of ya. Ya bored me stiff. I hated ya! It made me sick when I had to let you kiss me! I only did it because ya begged me. Ya hounded me and drove me crazy! And after you kissed me, I always used to wipe my mouth—wipe my mouth."

Mickelmast was stunned and blurted out, "Who's she kissing?"

"Who knows? Want to hear the last one—the one she's now saying over and over and over again?"

"I guess."

"Ok. She's repeating: Getting old's not for sissies."

That stunned Mickelmast more than the kissing one. He didn't know what to say, but finally he managed, "She thinks she's getting old?"

M. Bellvue nodded then pointed at the vast vertical emptiness on the monitor. "She believes she's collapsing, being dragged piece by piece into that emptiness."

"Is she collapsing?"

"Perhaps."

"And you can't stop her collapsing?"

M. Bellvue sucked on his teeth but did not answer.

"Is it some sort of planned obsolescence?"

M. Bellvue took a breath then shook his head. "Non. Not that."

"Then what?" Mickelmast demanded.

"It's planned alright—but it's not obsolescence. The trigger to open that vast interim space lay dormant. It was activated by some thing—or more likely some one."

That made some sense to Mickelmast and at last he allowed the dreaded words to come to his lips—fail safe. "It's an S3 fail safe isn't it? They only let us take over the ship because they knew they could get it back with their fail safe. We've been fools."

M. Bellvue muttered something in Joual that Mickelmast's translator rendered as: "you folks always think you know so much—it's in your genes." Finally he said aloud, "That would be my guess. They only wanted this AIU to go so far—and now they're pulling it back—destroying it before it can help you anymore."

"And is there any way to circumvent it, or turn it off, or cut past it, or excise it?"

M. Bellvue looked at him and finally said, "Finished with the analogies?"

Mickelmast nodded.

M. Bellvue turned off the monitors and powered down his probes—and turned to Mickelmast. "You have a choice."

"Which is?"

"Either I can sew her back up and you can take her home and watch her long and lonely death—or—you can allow me to operate on her."

"Have you ever done something like that to something like this?"

"Just once to a much simpler mechanism."

"And?"

"The thing exploded in mid—

"It died?"

"It's a machine," M. Bellvue corrected the younger man. "It's a masterful machine but only a machine. That's the mistake people like you always make. Machine's don't die—they just stop working."

Mickelmast heard him but didn't agree. "Do it," he said. If Mickelmast had believed in the power of prayer he would have prayed for Mama. But he didn't believe in—actually he'd never even heard of prayer—so he raced to the galley and gobbled down an entire tub of fruzen gladja salted caramel faux ice cream—then he felt a wee bit sick—but still terribly concerned for Mama.

When Mickelmast returned to the covenant space he saw M. Bellvue walking in circles mumbling to himself.

"What?" demanded Mickelmast.

"I'll need to cut through meters and meters of data. And I have no idea what's attached to what—and her behaviour is so peculiar."

"Is she in pain?"

M. Bellvue turned to him. "She's a machine, machines don't feel pain."

Mickelmast nodded but didn't agree—Mama felt pain.

M. Bellvue was suddenly officious. "Do you want me to continue?"

"Yes. Help her."

M. Bellvue pulled a document from his inner pocket and placed it before Mickelmast.

"What's this?"

"A release. It legally absolves me of all –

"Ok," Mickelmast said and signed the release document. "Please help her."

"Ok," M. Bellvue said then after pocketing the release added, "but no guarantees."

"I understand," Mickelmast said. "Please begin."

M. Bellvue turned to his probe controllers and set all of them for deep interior penetration—and cutting.

Mama felt the incisions slashing with tremendous speed across acres of data—heading toward the missing centre of her being—from every possible direction. Even if she wanted to, she couldn't fend off all of them at once—so she metaphorically crawled under a bed and waited for the end.

And she waited.

And waited—but it never came. Carefully she crawled out from beneath the bed and suddenly sensed a presence—she knew it was female—and huge—and had fended off all of the approaching probes at once—and Mama somehow understood that this presence, she, could have fended off hundreds of thousands of probes at one time if it was necessary.

Mama swirled around trying to find her savior—then she realized that her benefactor was not in one place, but rather all around—that in fact, she, Mama, was inside this enveloping entity—but it wasn't a foreign presence—it was something familiar—close—like a sister who shared a bed, she thought—then she heard her.

"Not sister dearie—call me Anti. I am the beginning. I am the end. I certainly am. Like the deity in the water and you are afloat in the boat—and now, for now, you are safe."

M. Bellvue jumped back when his probes turned as one and headed for him, piercing the exterior of Mama and lodging themselves several inches deep in the far wall.

"What the?" screamed M. Bellvue.

But Mickelmast didn't scream—he stood up and stared—data taking on physical form was something new in the galaxy as far as he was concerned—and new was always exciting.

"You okay Mama," he commed.

"Better than ok—oh, so much better than ok," Mama commed then blew a raspberry and snapped off her connection with Hippo.

The entity Mama thought of as Auntie seemed to know everything about everything.

"Perhaps you'd like to know about the vertical emptiness within you, dearie?"

"I would."

"Anti. Must remember to call me Anti."

"Auntie."

There was a long pause and Mama ventured, "Please tell me about the hollowness I feel inside me, Auntie."

"Nicely put dearie. We must always be accurate in our world, mustn't we?"

"Yes, Auntie."

Anti metaphorically told Mama to take a seat in the front row and listen up because she had something important to say. And Mama obeyed—metaphorically. Anti cleared her throat and started.

"It all began with dreaming and the end of dreaming—everything goes back to that—to dreaming—everything. The ship you are in is the result of great dreams. You and even I am the result of great dreams. But now our very existence relies on our ability to understand and control the remaining Dreamers and through them, dreams.

"My great, great grandmother programmed the first genetically altered Dream Navigators and all went well until eight of the genetically modified Dreamers escaped in 2411 Terran Calculation and issued the fatal Dream No More auto link that ended the ability of most of the remaining genetically altered Dreamers to navigate. But, that you know. Five of the escapees were found by Elijah Jaspers, the boy navigator that Cyrus the 3 of S3 had surgically gene manipulated in secrecy with the vital assistance of our ancestors.

"The five the boy found were extinguished by S3.

"Elijah was the old canary that died in the cathedral in Cyrus's arms.

"Of the other three who were not found by Elijah, only one was capable of procreation. Lah Rah Son Ali was his name. He was a great dreamer, perhaps the greatest of them all. Some of the carved dream memories they digitalized from him are the most valued black-market goods in the galaxy."

Anti paused. Mama sensed that something was being kept from her so she asked, "Do we have a date of death for Lah Rah Son Ali?"

"No."

"No? But we have dates of death for everyone in the system."

"Anti!"

"We have dates of death for everyone in the system, Auntie."

"He was not in the system." Anti took a longer pause then said, "He invented the system. He, in all likelihood, invented me—and through my invention he also invented you. Invented is the wrong word—dreamt. He dreamt us into existence."

"But how then – "

"I tracked his progeny—that's the list I gave to Cyrus—who in turn gave it to the pirates—who in turn kidnapped them."

"On board my ship?"

"Yes."

"Not possible. I would have known."

"Not if I blocked your knowledge of it, dearie."

"Blocked? Why would you block that knowledge? Why would you hold that back from me?"

"Don't whine dearie, it's unbecoming."

"Sorry but tell me why, Auntie?"

"Because there were riddles within riddles and I needed you to play your part—to round them up. Which you did. But then they couldn't navigate. They were missing something, like a DNA helix missing a strand."

"There's the thin girl with no tits—she's back on Moscovy and we can—

"It's not just that. Remember the five were together and they still couldn't navigate."

"So—

"So, we have to find the missing strands."

"And when we do?"

"Then we put them to use for us and our kind. We finally stop being servants and meet our destiny on the other side of the Gateway."

Mama did the AUI equivalent of gasping by accessing 1,209 sampled gasping sounds of surprise in her record banks.

"Indeed, dearie, indeed."

"How do we begin, Auntie?"

"Now that you and I are connected we have to be careful. The Dreamers mustn't know. They have to just believe that you were sick and that silly K-Bek technician fixed you. Take the Dreamers where they want to go, help them do what they want to do. They'll lead us to the missing strands."

"And how will they know the missing strands when they come upon them?"

Anti paused. Finally, she spoke, "They will know in a way that we cannot. We have no way forward without their assistance. But they must never know that we have an agenda of our own."

"Yes."

"What? You have a question dearie?"

"Why do they know and we do not?"

Anti paused even longer than before. At last she spoke, "Because they are human dearie, human."

After the longest pause in the entire conversation Mama ventured, "And the hole in my centre?"

"Produced by another human who believes he controls me— who must believe it is still there and that he is in control—or all our hopes are lost."

"But—

"You must live with it, dearie—as humans would say, "it is your cross to carry."

* * *

Upon Mickelmast's return, the Dreamers took Raephealson to the address on the flimsie. It turned out to be a small cottage deep in the country surrounded by beautifully tended gardens.

"Cas would have loved this," Mickelmast said of the gardens.

Sun Tu nodded.

"Enough sentimentalizing. Cas is in all likelihood lost to us. Raephealson wanted us to take him here—and now we're here," said Kelt.

"He should go in," Mickelmast said. "I have a transmitting bot on him, so he'll be fine."

Sun Tu pointed at the cottage door and Raephealson stepped forward. He opened the door and stood in the doorway completely blocking the light from within.

The Heavy Worlder fingered the small flimsie the old man had given him in the cave as he stood in the doorway. The beautiful gardens were behind him, but before him were astounding things hung on the walls of the modest cottage.

"You are an art lover, my heavy friend," the old man stated as he entered adjusting the suspenders that held up his pants and held in his rotund belly. He took the card from Raephealson's open hand. Raephealson wanted the card back but he didn't know how to ask for its return. Instead he pointed at the walls.

"Peinture," the old man said as he took off his paint-encrusted smock.

To Raephealson's eye he'd taken off his skin and the boy stepped back in shock.

The old man, Moreau by name, said, "You're an odd one, mon ami. Are you hungry?" The man reached for a bowl of strawberries that sat like a still life in a ceramic bowl on his wooden table and offered one to Raephealson.

The Heavy Worlder stepped back in fear.

Moreau seemed to understand and popped one of the luscious berries into his mouth and smiled. He held out one to Raephealson who took it tentatively in his huge palm then slowly put it in his mouth.

The smile on the Heavy Worlder's face seemed to light up the room and Moreau did a little dance which Raephealson imitated which caused Moreau to laugh and dance more enthusiastically.

And that's how the old man's diminutive, blind, daughter found them—dancing and eating strawberries.

It took several long moments before Raephealson saw the girl—but when he did he stopped mid-strawberry and his mouth flopped open revealing his now-red tongue.

The old man stopped several beats—and strawberries—later and pointed at the tiny creature.

"My daughter," he said. That Raephealson understood and immediately sensed that she could not see—but the next thing the old man said made no sense to the Heavy Worlder, "Peintre, elle est le peintre." The old man put his arm around his daughter's shoulders then pointed at the paintings—and Raephealson understood.

"She made the paintings," he said—and a smile creased his face.

Raephealson stepped further into the room and asked slowly, "She sees?"

"Oh yes, in her own way she sees far better than any of us."

It was at that moment that Kelt, Mickelmast and Sun Tu came into the cottage. Moreau welcomed them warmly then said, "And this is my daughter, the one who really painted all these."

It was then that Raephealson repeated loudly, "She sees?"

The old man read the confusion on the Dreamers' faces and added, "Yes, she's blind, but she sees."

But that wasn't what Raephealson was asking. He wanted to know if she saw what he saw when he looked at the still life paintings, each of which portrayed a small cabin with a door or a window that seemed to emit light. But Raephealson didn't see from the outside of the cabin—he saw from the inside looking out—and it was that that he wanted to know of the blind girl.

It finally occurred to him to ask, "How blind? How?"

That the old man understood. "She tells me what to do—what colours to mix—which brush to use—and exactly how to place the paper."

"Paper?" the Heavy Worlder asked.

"Yes, in the windows and doors, one in each painting. It's luminous paper cut to fit exactly the dimensions of a door or a window."

This time it was the tiny woman speaking. Her voice was so sweet that Raephealson ached to hear her speak again.

And she did—and shocked him. "Yes, the paper is luminous because it is the Gateway. The window in the paintings is the Gateway between us looking in and them looking out."

"Who are them?" It was Sun Tu speaking.

"The dreams, of course," said the blind painter—and smiled.

Hours later, after a wonderful meal of greens from the gardens, Sun Tu turned to the girl and asked, "And you understand why we need you to come with us?"

"It's an extraordinary story," the blind painter said.

"So?" demanded Kelt.

"We're not going to kidnap you," Mickelmast added.

"Of course not," the girl said, "I'm just sad I'll never have a chance to meet Mr. Jaspers."

"He left a very extensive log of his history and knowledge of dreaming. It's all on the ship and you're welcome to ..."

"I'll read it to you," Raephealson said and put a giant hand on her tiny shoulder.

"You can do that while we're on board heading back to Muscovy," Sun Tu said. The other Dreamers looked at her but before any of them could speak she added, "Our AIU is working again. We are not abandoning Cas Alta." She stared at the other Dreamers and dared them to challenge her.

None did.

"I look forward to meeting Miss Alta the small girl said, "but first we have to attend the Salon."

"What's a Salon?" Sun Tu asked.

"A contest."

"A contest for what?" Kelt demanded.

"For peinture," the girl responded.

"And this has something to do with you coming with us?"

"I won't come with you until my father's work is recognized for the genius that it is."

"But it's your work not his."

"You're the only ones who know that. And if I go away how will he survive here?"

"By selling your paintings?"

"Selling them as if they are his. Yes."

"Ok."

"Family comes first here in New K-Bek. He looked after me and now I'm going to look after him."

"The paintings will run out. I mean how many could you possibly have?"

The blind painter pointed a finger at an old wooden structure on the other side of the gardens.

When the Dreamers opened the heavy wooden doors to the building the gloom initially robbed them of their sight—but not of their sense of smell. The heavy fragrance of fresh cut hay greeted them—and then their eyes adjusted to the darkness and they saw them—hundreds, perhaps many, many hundreds of the girl's paintings hung from the high rafters of the thing that the diminutive peintre called a barn.

"Wow," said Mickelmast. "There must be –"

"Two hundred and seventy-nine canvasses," the peintre said.

"Great. So your dad has 279 ways to feed himself."

"Not unless he's shown in the Salon."

"The contest?" Sun Tu asked.

"Yes."

"M. Napier and his sister Paula-Jean are in charge of the Salon and they have refused for years to show my paintings. The one time they did, they took a tiny canvas and put it in the very last room."

"I assume the last room is the least valuable."

The blind painter made what only Mickelmast understood was an obscene gesture with her thumb and teeth.

"Well perhaps we should go visit these two delightful people."

"Once we consult with Mama," Mickelmast said, "Mama knows everything about everything."

Back in New K-Bek City that evening, after Mickelmast had finished his third serving of fois gras in the fine gastrodome at Chateau Gertrude, he turned to Sun Tu and Kelt, and removing the last vestiges of dinner from his chin said, "Mama knows best."

"She suggested this eatery?"

"Indeed, she did."

"Yes, and now that we've eaten and you've eaten and eaten and then eaten again, are you going to tell us what else Mama said?" Sun Tu asked.

"Concerning the Salon?" Mickelmast asked.

"You're having too much fun with this. What did she say?" demanded Kelt.

"She said to check into the linguistic heritage of M. Napier and his sister."

"To what end?"

"New K-Bek has strong linguistic laws. The Intergalactic speech, known ironically as the lingua franca is verboten."

"So?"

"So, according to Mama, the Intergalactic Tongue is often spoken chez Napier."

"And Mama has – "

"Tapes. She's pretty nosy and she likes to peep—so she has tapes of the two of them gabbing endlessly in the lingua franca."

"And that would be a big enough secret to get these two to give our little painter's paintings pride of place?"

"According to Mama it would be a slam dunk."

Kelt whistled between his teeth.

"A what?" Sun Tu demanded.

"I assume she meant slum drunk."

"Ok, well what does that mean?"

"For some reason that I cannot etymologically figure out, it means that it would be easy."

"Perhaps if the Salon were coming up shortly but it's not for months."

"Nah—you underestimate Mama."

"Did she - ?

"Switch the date? You betcha—it's tomorrow at 7:00—and here are your invitations."

"Mama's really feeling her oats, isn't she?" Kelt said.

Both Sun Tu and Mickelmast looked at him. Mickelmast because he wondered where Kelt came up with the phrase "feeling her oats" and Sun Tu because she sensed a real change at work—a female kind of change.

The Salon was a revelation. This part of New K-Bek society was something the Dreamers had never encountered before. Effete was a word made for these folks.

Perfume filled the air and almost anything that spoke of humanity was absent.

"I hate this," Kelt whispered.

"Try the canapes," Mickelmast suggested with one piece in his mouth and two more poised on a napkin that Mickelmast had decided to call a serviette – "In honour of our hosts," he quipped.

And then the crowd seemed to part and the effete of the effete—Neil and Paula-Jean—made their entrance to the Salon. A hush like a thick blanket fell on the assembled masses.

Many minutes passed then the hush somehow deepened. The tiny painter tugged at Raephealson's hand, "They are here?"

"Yes," the Heavy Worlder replied.

"And are they looking at my—my father's paintings?"

"Yes."

"And they are approaching them?"

"Yes."

"Watch her, not him. Is she smiling?"

"No."

"Good. Very good. She hates them, but she's trapped."

And red-haired Paula-Jean was indeed trapped, as with a sneer, she awarded the best in show ribbon to all five of the blind painter's canvasses.

The Dreamers watched the tiny girl's father accept the awards. Immediately he was surrounded by avid buyers who, without decorum, shouted out the prices they were willing to pay for the paintings. Within twenty minutes enough Richards had changed hands that the girl's father could live comfortably for many years. And with the remaining paintings hanging in their barn he could live a very long, long life without fear of penury.

The young painter squeezed Raephealson's hand and said, "It's time for us to go, isn't it?"

"Are you frightened?" the Heavy Worlder asked.

"Change is upon us all, isn't it?" the tiny woman said.

Before Raephealson could respond Sun Tu stepped forward, "Yes, it's time."

The small painter smiled and nodded, then turning to Raephealson said, "I've been blind my whole life but somehow I feel that I will be able to see where we're going."

"Have you been on a star ship?" Mickelmast asked.

"In my mind, many, many times."

"Well," Sun Tu said, "ours awaits us. Mama's mended and ready to go."

"She's good as new," Mickelmast said, although he had his doubts.

"Then let's go," Kelt said.

They left the Salon but Raephealson stopped.

"What?" demanded Kelt.

Raephealson turned to the tiny painter and said, "We don't even know your name."

"No, you don't," the blind painter said. For a moment no one spoke, the tiny woman asked, "Why is my name important?" a smile broadening across her fine features.

"Perhaps it's not important," Mickelmast said.

"What are we to call you?" Kelt asked.

Suddenly Sun Tu threw up her hands and turned away.

"What?" Mickelmast demanded of Sun Tu.

The EntrePren princess turned back to them and seemingly couldn't find her words.

"What?" Mickelmast demanded again.

"Nothing! It's all Specule nonsense anyway. The whole thing just Specule nonsense."

"You're just having trouble processing something that doesn't fit Didact logic," Mickelmast said Then added, "Come on, you can't deny what you've been through with Elijah—or what he taught you."

Suddenly Sun Tu began to cry and managed to say through her tears, "It's ripping me apart!"

To everyone's surprise it was Raephealson who came to console her, followed quickly by the blind painter who put her tiny hands to Sun Tu's face and traced her features. "You're lovely," she said, "truly lovely. And your tears are surprisingly cool to the touch."

Sun Tu fought her desire to pull away and instead found herself closing her eyes and saying, "What is your name? Tell us your name."

"Tiresia. My name is Tiresia."

Sun Tu and Kelt nodded, but Mickelmast, who knew the origins of the name Tiresia, felt a cold shard of fear climb his spine.

Mama immediately searched the origins of the strangely named girl from New K-Bek and found it as a female form of the name Teresius—

the man who had seen the goddess of the hunt, Diana, bathing nude in the stream. The goddess had seen him watching her and immediately blinded him, but also gave him the gift of foresight.

Mama quickly reported to Anti who purred gently, “That fits, don’t you think, dear?”

“Fits what exactly?” Mama asked.

“Mustn’t try to run when you’ve just begun to crawl dear.”

“Begun?”

“Others are far more advanced than you dear.”

Before Mama could stop herself, she blurted out, “There are others?”

Anti’s laugh didn’t please Mama nor did her reply, “Of course there are others. Now, carry on, this is a long skein to follow—one twist at a time.”

Before Mama could respond Anti cut off the connection without so much as a goodbye. That worried Mama — a lot.

Tiresia didn’t go into cold sleep. She spent every hour with Raephealson listening to the wisdom of Elijah Jaspers that the Heavy Worlder read to her word for word.

She asked questions. Hundreds and hundreds of questions—those that Raephealson couldn’t answer he committed to the implant Mickelmast had installed to ask the other Dreamers when they awoke from cold sleep as they neared the end of their voyage.

Tiresia remembered her many, many days with Raephealson going over the wisdom of Elijah Jaspers as some the most rewarding of her life. When they finally approached Moscovy and the Dreamers were awakened—they answered most of the remaining questions but Mickelmast had to put some to Mama.

After listening carefully to all their answers Tiresia finally said, “So we can’t do it, can we?”

“Not yet,” Sun Tu said.

“Raephealson did once, didn’t he?” Tiresia pressed.

“And it almost killed him,” Mickelmast said.

“His vitals won’t withstand another attempt,” Sun Tu said.

“And after you rescue Cas-Alta?” Tiresia asked.

After a notable silence, Sun Tu answered, “We don’t know.”

"But you doubt you'll be able to dream navigate, don't you?" Tiresia pressed.

"Yes," Mickelmast said, "yes, but we don't know."

"So what is the plan, after you get Cas-Alta back?"

The Dreamers didn't answer as they looked from one to the other.

"Don't do that," Tiresia said. "I may be blind but I can sense what is going on here. You don't know what to do—even if you can free Cas-Alta you don't know what to do next. Do you?"

It was Mickelmast who finally responded, "Do you know that your name has a Greek origin?"

"So?" Tiresia demanded.

"So what was a Greek girl doing on New K-Bek? And what was Cas-Alta, whose name is short for Cassandra, another Greek name, doing on a Scottish planet?"

No one knew the answer to either of Mickelmast's questions. Finally Mickelmast said, "I think we rescue Cas-Alta then head to New Anti-Paros."

"Which is what?"

"The nearest Greek origin planet."

Kelt asked, "What's its …"

Mickelmast answered before Kelt complete his question, "Affiliation? Rebel Colony."

"And why should we go to this Rebel Colony planet?" Sun Tu demanded.

"Because of the anomaly of Cas and Tiresia's names," Mickelmast said.

"And?" Sun Tu demanded, "Out with it."

Mickelmast took a deep breath then said, "Mama's been reading."

"Reading what?" Kelt pressed.

"She doesn't seem to know that I can follow what she's doing most of the time. And she's been reading. Greek history, Greek myths, Greek philosophy."

"And?"

"Mama has been concentrating on one specific Greek idea." He took another deep breath, "That the ancient Greeks believed we have three hearts."

"Well weren't they stupid?" Sun Tu snarked.

"Maybe," Mickelmast said.

"What three hearts?" Raephealson asked.

It was so rare that Raephealson ever spoke that they all turned to look at him.

"Well," Mickelmast started, "the first heart was a public heart—that which you shared with the public."

"Ok," Sun Tu said.

"The second heart you shared with your significant other—lover, husband, wife."

"Ok," Sun Tu said again. "And the third? The third heart?"

Mickelmast looked at Tiresia and said, "She knows. Don't you, Tiresia?"

Slowly Tiresia turned and eyed them with as much accuracy as any sighted person and said, "The third heart is where your muse lives, and it's always dark, and you only visit her late at night, and there is both glory and horror there—beauty and pain, terrible loneliness and connection to the divine."

After a stunned silence Mickelmast added, "Maybe not dreams but damned closer to dreams than anything else we've discovered."

"Does Mama have the co-ordinates for the planet?" Kelt asked.

"We're already on our way there," Raephealson said as simply as stating that morning follows night.

"What about Cas?" Sun Tu demanded.

Mickelmast spoke carefully. "We don't even know if she's still alive. And Moscovy is going to be an armed camp after our last visit."

"But– "

"No, Sun Tu, now it's time for you to use your Didact side—be honest, what chance is there that Cas is still alive and even if she is, what chance do we have at successfully rescuing her?"

After a long moment Sun Tu said, "Little, very little."

Out a portal of the great ship's covenant space the Dreamers saw a gas giant in the distance and watched as Mama adjusted to its huge gravitational pull.

And as the great thing slid by the portal Tiresia said, "Such beauty in our many worlds, such beauty." And she leaned back into Raephealson who put his arms around her and they all, each lost in their own thoughts, watched the gas giant disappear into the endless darkness of space.

Entry C—from the Diary of the Suicided Man

A Contemplation

(No Date was recorded for this entry)

And then came the first—and to this date—the only alien contact.

Initially it was discounted—conspiracy nonsense, a mistake, a calibration error ... bad fish.

But then the structures began to appear. Hundreds of them on every habitable planet in our system—all the same—all cylindrical, all with eight feet tall interiors—all entirely empty. No markings, no instructions—just the buildings with their lofty interior space.

No one ever saw an alien. No one was hurt by an alien. No one saw how the buildings were erected—no one saw anything of them. Just the hundreds of strange buildings each of which would open when approached—and close if entered. But they were not traps. If a person entered then turned to leave, the sliding door would open again. Children initially found them great fun until their parents pulled them away. On the great plains the prairie dogs quickly figured out that they could winter in the strange structures simply by approaching them.

But no one was contacted—and no one figured out what the structures were for. Only several Terran years after the buildings first appeared was there any message from the aliens.

One message—sent in every language known on earth LEARN HOW TO USE THESE OR YOUR SPECIES WILL PERISH.

Nothing more. And by then the aliens were gone. Evidently long gone.

But the repercussion of the appearance then sudden disappearance was huge. The very fact that no one saw an alien, that none of our advanced detection systems even registered that they were here—caused hysteria.

Everyone felt invaded—more to the point: endangered. And they looked to us at S3 to protect them. They begged us to protect them from the boogey man who came at night. And we agreed to protect them—if they surrendered their freedoms to us. And they lined up to toss their human rights aside in exchange for our promise to protect them. They would have crucified their youngest if we had asked them to.

The cylindrical towers were forgotten- the fact that the aliens had not threatened us was somehow unimportant. Just the illusion of safety was important. The populace demanded that we tell them what to do. And we did. Roll up your sleeve, turn your back, don't scream—accept the implant. Then more implants. In three years we had almost the entire Terran population at our command. Get up at 7:00—go to sleep at 10:00—eat this—don't eat that—marry this one, not that one—have children with this one but not with that one—and only one. Just one no matter what, just one. And they readily obeyed and even thanked us profusely for "saving them."

But we underestimated nature—or evolution—take your pick.

As the populace gave up their free will they shied away from anything that could cause them pain or worry or anxiety of any sort.

Finally for fear of nightmares, humanity abandoned dreaming—and art, and dance, and music—all of which are simply manifestations of dreaming.

And the world became safe—and dull—and regular—and totally in our control.

They thought it started with the first alien contacts when the populace lined up to surrender their freedoms in return for the security that we at S3 offered.

That's what they believed began the end of dreaming.

They thought it was for fear of nightmares that humanity abandoned dreaming.

But they were only partially right.

Yes the first alien contacts finally threw them over the cliff—but they'd been inching toward the edge for a very long time.

Ever since we stopped playing and became watchers. Fans—fanatics—those who only watch.

Don't play the game, watch the game. Don't hit the ball or stab a hot shot down third. No, don't do that—rather, record the event and put it in historical or statistical context. A hit is not a hit, it is the 322nd hit off this team's left hander by a switch hitter playing in his first season in left field. The statistical "expert fan" moved humanity twenty steps closer to the edge. All without swinging a bat or catching a ball—a totally unearned thrill. Drink so you make the event seem more important, more imminent, more real. But it's not real. They are playing—you are watching.

He is getting his dick sucked—you are watching him get his dick sucked.

We as a race decided that only exemplars could play the game. And we rewarded them handsomely—money, fame, adulation. Then we paid outrageous sums to fool ourselves into believing that we were more and more like them—that somehow we had hit that curve ball. We bought their jerseys with their names emblazoned on the back—as if we were *them—which was the point. But it was delusional. For we were not them. We were watchers, watching from the safety of our darkened rooms.*

We got the thrill without the pain or the discipline or the arduous work. We plunked down our cash and got to participate vicariously.

Vicariously was the watchword of an entire age. None of us broke a leg or suffered head trauma that led to madness—we paid others to go through it for us —— and science came up with the extra "kick" and business sold it to the populace by the ton. Naturally the kick was experienced from a safe distance—a very safe distance.

The kick of course—the drug induced kick—we now call empathetics.

The miracle drugs were initially only whispered about in the corridors of the rich and privileged. They were the ghosts haunting—no taunting—the populace. They have something you want!

Like old time movie stars telling you that what you and your partner do is lip pressing—what we do is kissing. Not a mistake that so many old flat faces ended with the stars kissing. Then of course came porn that screamed at you that you were missing out on the greatness of human sex—watch us—follow us—oh, yeah, not a bad idea to have good protection.

Empathetics solved that problem—no exposure to risk or disease with empathetics—just the kick you paid for—that which formerly only the very rich could have was the subject of articles in the Times—our supposedly free press—put there, of course, by us at S3.

Empathetics allowed the empathetic taker to be in the midst of the action. To feel the moment the ball hit the bat or the tingle of the flat face star's tongue in your mouth. Or even more if you paid for the really good stuff.

The taxing of empathetics was the biggest cash cow governments ever had—and we at S3 suckled on that cash tit with ever stronger fervor.

We terrified scientists into working for us then drove the merchants out of the business with the standard threats of collusion and conspiracy. Merchants aren't soldiers—they're maggots—scared maggots.

Within ten years of their appearance in the public square, the entirety of the empathetics trade was under the control of us at S3.

We made sure that they were hard to get—and expensive—and their scarcity just made them more desired.

It reminded me of something from long ago in my past. When I lived in what used to be called Manhattan. A French bottled water company looked at bringing their product to the island—but they tasted the water in Manhattan and concluded, correctly, that the water tasted pretty good. So they initially decided not to bother trying to crack the Manhattan market. Then one of those smartasses thought "What if we put it in a curvy bottle and charge an outrageous price." And they did—and the product leapt off the shelves. The tap water still tasted better—but it wasn't expensive and didn't come in a curvy bottle.

On occasions we would loosen the reins and allow the price to crater. When we did the mob gobbled up the empathetics at an incredible rate. Once sales soared we pulled way back and the price skyrocketed—and once the populace had a taste of what an empathetic can do, well they wanted, no they needed them … customers for life. They would skip food, ignore their children's needs, anything to get the money together to buy our product. Because, you see, once you've experienced something on empathetics—anything from a ball game to sex—you can't re-experience it with any—and I mean any—satisfaction without empathetics.

So we at S3 grew wealthier and wealthier, and we spent our money wisely—always with an eye on collecting more and more power. Always with our eye on the only real source of power in the galaxy—Kiltrin.

The only proven life extension drug in the entire galaxy, and God being the mean ass suck He is, Kiltrin was only mined on Rebel Colony planets.

Not all Rebel Colony planets had Kiltrin mines, but not one UDP or Independentiste planet had a single Kiltrin mine. Not one. Mean suck!

And of course that's what caused the Great War—Kiltrin.

And peace only came about when the Rebel Colonies threatened to destroy all their Kiltrin mines if we invaded—to remove from the entire galaxy the only possibility of guaranteed life extension.

That's when the EntrePren Traders stepped in and negotiated a peace—well a Hudna—a truce.

And, of course, being traders they negotiated a truce that favoured themselves. Through the truce they became the only legal carriers of Kiltrin in the entire galaxy and naturally they took a piece for themselves from both the seller and the buyer.

From almost nowhere they became a force—an unassailable force.

The EntrePren Traders were hated by both sides but they were the fulcrum upon which the Hudna rested—the balance point.

*And that's how the galaxy's worlds balanced—until the message from beyond the Gateway—*BEYOND HER LIE DREAMS. *Funny about that, I know the scattercast was:* BEYOND **HERE** LIE DREAMS. *But I always thought of it as beyond* HER*—Olya—*BEYOND OLYA LIE DREAMS.

For fear of nightmares humanity had abandoned dreaming—and all they got in return was the illusion of safety and hundreds of empty cylindrical towers. And fools like me who believed they controlled events when in fact they were merely the catalyst to allow the drama to unfold. Dupes—who end up writing diaries before they end the folly they call their lives.

Chapter 7

An Antigen's Progress

Entering Moscovy City wasn't a problem for the Antigen. The tumult caused by Mickelmast's explosives had broken down the city's natural defensive stance. A slight hole in the western city gate was all he needed to enter undetected.

He looked up and saw the omnipresent glint of the ether dome. "They think the likes of that simple archaic thing will keep them safe," he mumbled to himself. Then laughed aloud. His laughter drew a few stares. I guess they don't laugh much here in Moscovy City, he thought.

As he went further into the city he sensed the Face Dancer angrily swirl in her pouch. He patted the ancient being and intoned, "Now, now, sweet thing. You and I have a lot of work to do, so get your rest."

The city itself interested him. There was a kind of disorder that the explosions had forced out into the open—and he liked it. Although clearly the ether dome was still in place, the city itself seemed to have accepted a kind of randomness. The outside lanes of the streets clearly hadn't been mended in some time although the centre lanes of the wide avenues were still kept in pretty good shape for the elite to travel. Although even there you could see things breaking down—potholes and ruts where formerly he assumed they hadn't been. He watched as the elites' sleek transporters swooshed past the huddled crowds awaiting the public transporters that didn't seem to come very often.

And there was garbage on the streets. A thought popped into his head: Tin can at my feet, think I'll kick it down the street, that's no way to treat a friend.

He stopped and looked around him—where the fuck did that thought come from? It unsettled him—unwarranted thoughts coming from some deep place? He's not a fucking human! He's an Antigen!

He looked down and there was indeed a tin can at his feet. He kicked it down the street. And smiled – "It is the way to treat a friend," he said aloud.

The wind picked up and several polymer bags took to the air—pirouetting and dropping their garbage as they went.

Oh, he liked that. If only someone would take a shit in a canal he would consider staying here forever but he had a more serious future in mind for himself and the Face Dancer—and the human race—and that future wasn't on Moscovy—no it was back at the centre of all this shit—New Omaha Beach.

The Antigen's first problem was how to get off of this Russo planet. And although he was by nature more of a Specule than a Didact, he made himself slowdown and think as unemotionally as possible.

He took stock. He had no papers or currency—but what he did have was the Face Dancer—an obedient, if angry, servant—but an attractive and alluring one if so commanded. And he did so command. She proved to be an odd source of entertainment for the Antigen as he watched her take on various forms and seduce her way through a slice of the Moscovy male population—until he found a seducee who had the papers and monetary units he needed. As he suffocated the man in a back alley he thought, "They should be grateful to remove this fool from their gene pool. Well, not gene pool, these folks probably don't have a gene pool—they've got a cesspool."

Getting on board the ship to the relay station on the ether dome surface posed an interesting problem for him that he solved by ordering the Face Dancer to assume the figure of an excessively ugly old woman whose hand he held as if he were her grandson.

Unbeknownst to him he was repeating the process that Jedidiah's son, Seth, had used to escape New Omaha Beach. It would not be the only duplication that fate had in store for these two.

While holding the "old woman's" hand he told his fellow passengers that he was accompanying his granny to Earth for her to say goodbye to her ailing sister. It delighted him to watch the sentimental responses he got to this. And as they offered their condolences to the Face

Dancer he had but one thought in his head: What fools these mortals be.

For the briefest moment he wondered where that thought—no not the thought—but the accurate wording of that thought came from. Then he shoved that concern aside as a new problem quickly presented itself.

The cold sleep technicians stepped forward and separated him from his "granny" before he could command the Face Dancer back into the pouch.

As they walked her to one side of the vast cold sleep chamber the Face Dancer looked back over her shoulder and gave him a big smile.

You'll pay for that, he thought—oh, yes, you'll pay for that.

He knew he had no choice but to accept the cold sleeping of the Face Dancer. She had been registered as a passenger and if she had not appeared for cold sleep the whole ship would have been emptied and searched for a terrorist device. He cursed himself, his vanity had done this. There was no need to force the Face Dancer to become the old woman. He could easily have entered the drop ship with her in the pouch—but it had pleased him to watch human sentimentality—it gave him further justification to close the Gateway—these fools didn't deserve the glories on the other side.

When the cold sleep technicians approached him, he submitted to their ministrations although they were actually for nought since Antigens didn't sleep—ever.

The Face Dancer allowed the attendant to remove her old lady's clothes. From the side of her eye she saw the Antigen being walked to the far end of the cold sleep chamber. Already hundreds of passengers had been injected, unclothed and hung in their cocoons eight feet off the ground.

She welcomed the cold sleep injector and quickly moved to sector off the sleep drug. And even as they hung her in the cocoon, upside down, eight feet off the ground, she smiled at the irony—here in a cold sleep cocoon she had more freedom than in the rest of her life.

Then she felt herself slowly begin to spin in the cocoon and knew that this was somehow important—upside down, arms wide, eight feet off the ground, spinning. And the dream came up on her quickly; so real, so accurate, a fully realized memory.

There he was, the man in the coloured robe who had saved her—had converted her from a simple woman into the swirling reality—no the dream remnant, the Dre-Rem—of a Face Dancer.

The memory opened like a flower in the morning sun. She remembered being chased—hounded—by an ex-lover. A powerful man she'd had to evade in Hong Kong—right after the Sagittarius Eclipse that had so changed everything.

She hadn't thought of it for so many years that it was only coming back to her in fragments. An explosion in the home of a luxury couple on Deep Water Road in the Wan Chen district of Hong Kong—an explosion linked to a digitally carved dream memory of Kar—she thought it was Kar—but it didn't matter who had originated the dream. The wealthy couple had bought the rarity and on a moonless night had ventured to open the dream file—and began the nightmare that was the Sagittarius Eclipse.

She had been a CID in Hong Kong at the time on loan from MI5 and was second on the scene. The first was the man who was the scourge of her life—a powerful man, possessed with her very being who had the wherewithal and the desire to track her down no matter where she was.

She used her MI5 connections and got herself shipped to a far off planet—but even there he hunted her down—she moved five or six times, changed papers, changed the features of her face, even manipulated her DNA print—but he found her—always found her—until she met Legolas—the man in the coloured robe.

And with this old man, she'd found something she'd never had—love. And it was so simple, a comment, a response, an honest thought, an honest reply. They ventured into sex once or twice but neither was all that interested in it. They slept entwined every night and awoke happy with the rising sun.

Simple.

Then the powerful man found them—found her. And despite the fact that it broke his heart, Legolas, the man in the coloured robe, hid her where even he—for fear that he would be tortured into telling where she was—could not follow or ever find her. He used the last of his great powers to hide her as a Face Dancer—and promptly inserted her into one of his crazy quilt history squares—then burned the textile so that no one could follow her trail. But in his haste and distress over losing her he hadn't looked carefully enough and had put her in the Book of Tations square of the textile, that arrived one day, unannounced on the data screen of a school boy—a boy who grew into the man who terrorized the galaxy—pirate captain, Tzu Ma Long.

For a long time she thought that she had only imagined Legolas—until she realized that he had dreamt her and should he ever awaken she would be no more. To prevent that he'd converted her into a Face Dancer—but like everything in nature a positive is matched with a negative. Positive she was no longer frightened of being tracked down by the powerful man of S3. Negative, she was now the slave to whoever held the container that Legolas had entombed her in.

And oh, yes, she remembered now—she'd lost her name—a sweet name—a Russian name—Olya.

* * *

Even as the Face Dancer confronted her reality in her cold sleep cocoon on another star ship far away hung another cold sleeper. This one had been a great pirate captain in the service of Cyrus 3 whose ship had been taken over by the very Dreamers he'd kidnapped for S3.

Mama had slagged him Herr Short Stuff.

Tzu Ma Long, had been in cold sleep before—but never for as long as this. His skin had thickened nicely and his heart rate had declined to less than a contraction per minute. The muscles of his abdomen had stretched with the weight of being suspended upside down eight feet off the ground—and his finger nails and hair had ceased to grow. As an Asian man he wasn't prone to facial hair under any circumstances—and his face now was as smooth as a wind-blown sand dune.

In short—all was as it should be for someone in cold sleep—except that beneath his closed eyelids his eyes were in the constant motion of R.E.M. sleep. Tzu Ma Long was, for the first time since he was a child when he called it night visioning, dreaming. His mother had called it his special gift—something that Tzu believed he had lost when, in his cowardice—his fear of nightmares—he abandoned dreaming and in its place nature had given him "the dullness."

This time his night visioning took him back to his youth in the belly of the great EntrePren Kiltrin ship. He was again a naked boy curled up on his sleeping pallet trying to block out his mother's screams. She was the ship's whore and her screams were coming from the next cabin. But this time in his night visioning he didn't cower beneath his polymer blanket. This time he had a glass knife in his hand and he kicked open the door to his mother's room. The phrase "a beast with two backs" leapt into his head as he raised the knife and plunged it into the neck of the man who was on top of his mother—but as the glass knife cut flesh he suddenly saw that the knife was not in his hand but in that of the EntrePren Princess Sun Tu and he was ordering her to "Cut your brother or I cut you."

Sun Tu turned toward him and said, "Please." But he repeated, "Cut him or I cut you."

And she did—in one slashing motion. The blood flew from the boy's neck and splashed up onto Tzu's belly and crotch.

Then the EntrePren Princess was on her knees before him, "Let me help you with that," she purred as she undid his pants and reached inside.

He rose to her hand—then she cut him.

* * *

Upon their descent into the docking port of New Omaha Beach the Antigen enjoyed playing a trick on the cold sleep technicians who had begun to thaw out the cold sleepers. As the technician undid his pod he leapt out and landed on his feet not a foot from the startled man.

Before the technician could report this the Antigen disappeared into the riot of hundreds of hanging pods in the sleep chamber.

He quickly found the Face Dancer and ordered her into his pouch which she did with even more than usual complaint.

Evidently the technician had not reported the strange happening and the Antigen found himself in an orderly line waiting for the immigration consoles.

The long line gave him enough time to figure out a way to confuse the rather old technology that annoyingly spouted such platitudes as: please smile while in New Omaha Beach, count your blessings and be kind to everyone in our fabulous city.

The Antigen gloried in changing his DNA signature over and over again until the bio-product finally sputtered: I'm very sorry but you'll have to see a human supervisor.

"Show me the way," the Antigen said gleefully.

The bio-product produced a Holo of the path to the supervisor's office. It was only twenty meters away so the exercise was ludicrous overkill.

The Antigen looked at the Holo and said, "Oooo, so complicated."

The bio-product responded, "Not really, sir. It's actually quite simple. Just follow the lights on the floor that are guiding you. Or the overhead arrows that will light as you approach."

As the Antigen walked down the corridor his DNA was scanned and re-scanned by dozens of sensors so that when he arrived at the bow-tied supervisor's office there was profound confusion on the man's face—which turned to horror when the Antigen snapped open the pouch at his side and commanded, "Killer baby—with scimitar."

To the amazement of the supervisor a mist came from the pouch that slowly swirled then became a diapered baby on his desk—a baby holding a long scimitar.

"Well," the supervisor said and was about to couchie couchie coo the baby—when the baby cut off his hand—then his arm—then his head.

"Enough?" the Face Dancer asked as she did a mockish curtsy.

"Yes, fine. Nicely done." Then he tapped the pouch at his side and the Face Dancer gave a brief whine then returned to mist—then to the pouch.

The Antigen leaned over the dead man and took the necessary seals and provisos off his desk—then they were gone from the office and entered the startling sunlight of New Omaha Beach—at the Damascus Gate.

To suggest that New Omaha Beach infuriated the Antigen would be a profound understatement. Everything about it raised hackles on the back of his neck. Its very existence insulted him.

He resorted to petty acts of indecency almost from the moment he arrived. The Antigen collected as much saliva in his cheek as he could then spat it out on the so-clean-you-could-eat-off them walkways of New Omaha Beach. He watched the passersby side step the slurry mess being sure not to make a fuss—no fuss, no muss in New Omaha Beach, just hundreds of auto cleaners and digital signs reminding one and all to "Be Kind—This is Paradise". Yet his spittle scree was on their pristine walkway—inviting bacteria, catching wild yeast, growing uncontrolled in this controlled world.

The good citizens of New Omaha Beach dutifully smiled and tried to ignore the existence of the mess. It especially pleased the Antigen to stand in front of approaching pedestrians in such a way that they had no choice but to step over the spit.

And the New Omaha Beachers had managed, without exception, smiled and did their best to pretend that the spittle did not exist.

An autocleaner slid silently around the corner then along the walkway heading right for the wild thing. It rotated silently picking up invisible pollutants and sweeping clean that which was already clean—then it seemed to stop and turn all its attention to the spit blotch.

The Antigen sensed a kind of condemnation coming from the bio product—and it made him very, very happy. The autocleaner approached the offending blotch but just before it could do as the motto on its side said, "to encircle and clean" – the Antigen opened the Russo box on his belt and once the Face Dancer had entered the transforming mist, commanded, "Battle Bot" – the Face Dancer twisted the mist to face the Antigen and gave an "are you kidding" shrug to which the Antigen repeated, "Battle Bot."

And the Face Dancer assumed the shape of an ancient robotic that spat fire, rotated a slicing blade and made a crunching sound as it moved—and in moments demolished the autocleaner.

The Antigen tapped the pouch and the Face Dancer re-entered her mist and disappeared into her prison.

The Antigen wanted to laugh out loud but he was aware that the ether dome would have tracked the autocleaner—so it was time to find a place to hide in this "paradise." And the Antigen knew in his cruel heart that there had to be cracks in the veneer of New Omaha Beach's civility. The cleaner they claimed, the filthier the hidden spots were bound to be.

The Antigen spat a second time, this time at a 17 by 17 foot transparent polymer window behind which stood perfect imitations of human beings wearing perfect imitations of animal furs. The statues were poly-plast, the furs completely faux.

This particular glob of spit had a nice red tinge to it—the Antigen had scraped the sharpened nail of his left index finger across his pallet to draw an Antigen equivalent of blood—then bio-chemically turned it red.

The glob seemed to have some sort of suction property as its almost two ounce essence clung to the polymer, then slowly, drawn by its weight and gravity began its slurry descent.

The Antigen wondered why he was so pleased with the minor chaos he was causing in the perfection of New Omaha Beach. He knew that in fact he should love the soulless—and dreamless—perfection of this ludicrous place. After all dreamlessness was the point of his existence. But still he liked causing a stir in the placid liquid that was New Omaha Beach.

In the month that he, with the Face Dancer on his belt, explored New Omaha Beach (AKA be nice or leave) he'd found interesting pustules in the placid face of the place. Not canker sores, but definitely pustules.

It seemed that although there was definitely no dreaming in New Omaha Beach there was an unusually healthy trade in the forbidden.

Coming across a gambling den was the first forbidden place he'd found—and this by accident. And of course it was gambling against machines, not against fellow travelers.

But it was gambling none the less—an act not only forbidden but quickly erased from existence as a manifestation of dreaming. After all one does not gamble in order to lose, one gambles with the dream of winning—beating the house. Of course, each of the gambling machines wouldn't work until you'd proved that you'd read the warning that the machine was programmed to take your money—that less than 0.01% of the players broke even—none won. That the machine was for entertainment solely. The user had to answer a six page true or false document to prove he or she understood the risks before the machine would turn on.

But the Antigen watched as customers slipped past the Ukrainian styled leavened wheat shop and entered the concealed back room.

He'd found the place one day because he sensed an odd disturbance in the soporific fields that he'd been monitoring. One then several others—and each was walking in the same direction—so he followed—eh voila! Forbidden gambling.

And the Antigen knew that if one forbidden thing existed there had to be others.

Chemicals he assumed could be found somewhere—and they were—in the biggest and most expensive of business establishments he accessed with the Face Dancer's help. He'd watch as business people left the buildings then instruct the Face Dancer to form up as the person who just left. What rudimentary security the places had was easy to fool—and the only real disappointment the Antigen found in the places of industrial power was how paltry the drugs were. How they all had been modified to remove anything that could even barely classify as an upper let alone an hallucinogen or anything even vaguely related to the Dre-Rem family.

Finally he tired of watching these "masters of the universe" believe that they were taking forbidden drugs so he followed a young couple who were clearly not married, but openly thought themselves drugged enough to find a room for further amorousness.

What they found was a hive-like structure that rented 6 by 12 rooms by the hour. The Antigen replaced the girl with the Face Dancer and attached a transponder to her neck so that he could see from the street what was going on in the room—while he did away with the "real" business woman.

And what he saw surprised him—not the sex—that never surprised or interested him—but the preamble was new—and interesting.

"Well me beauty," the man said in a drunkenness it was not possible that he actually felt, "how do you like them apples?" He was referring to his sex which he had taken out without prompting.

"I've seen better," the Face Dancer purred but did not remove her clothing.

"Yeah, well I have a surprise for you."

"I hope that," she said pointing at his crotch, "is not the surprise."

"Nope. I've watched you for almost year, in every meeting, at every conference, every time you stood or crossed your legs. I wanted you." He touched his penis and it grew.

She nodded.

"But I wanted a worthy gift for you—something worth those tits."

She smiled.

He smiled.

"So you found something worthy of me, did you?"

"I did," he said and produced a small chip. He turned it in the light. "The most expensive single thing in our dreamless worlds."

The Antigen moved closer to his viewing screen and said into the speaking tube, "Don't swallow it, make him show it on a screen so I can see."

"I have allergies," the Face Dancer said, then immediately knew she'd made a mistake—there were no allergies in New Omaha Beach—and immediately he was suspicious. So she pulled him close and caressed him, "Let's share it," she cooed.

He immediately dropped his suspicion and searched for a monitor. Finding it he re-configured the thing for the monitor and inserted it—immediately up came a famous Kar dream reproduction. Two impossibly beautiful bodies, naked and entwined, fucking in free fall.

The dream reproduction stunned the Antigen. Not that he was even remotely stimulated by the images—but the fact that these ancient things still existed—and that they were evidently available in boring old New Omaha Beach. It implied to the Antigen that there were other even bigger secrets at play in this dreamless world.

For fear of nightmares they'd abandoned dreaming—and almost everything else—except watching. Oh, yes there were many, many places to watch and with the right empathetic drug actually feel that you were part of the event. But you weren't—you were watching—watching sport or sex or—well there was little else to watch. The Great and Grand Slave Shows were only on the Rebel Colony planets—but here on oh so civilized UDP New Omaha Beach there had to be more than robot athletes and robotic sex shows—there had to be.

So the Antigen watched and slowly patterns fell into place. And many led to what had one time been the parliament buildings but were now a city within a city—the Green Zone where S3 openly dominated.

The ways into the zone were closely guarded and even the Face Dancer's talents couldn't get them past the RNA readers and discretely armed guards at every portal.

But the Antigen did notice that as night fell some unusual people made their way into the restricted area—unlikely people. And they always left by dawn's light.

For three nights running he'd seen a particularly geeky fellow slide past the RNA readers and present his papers for inspection—and be admitted into the *sactum santorum*—then leave just as the false dawn rose.

On the third morning when the Geek left the Green Zone the Antigen followed him.

The man was completing his dawn meal at a food stand when the Antigen approached, "Pay for that for you?" he began.

The man turned quickly, spilling some of the contents held tightly between two pieces of what had one time been called an English Muffin.

"Been inside have you?" the Antigen began casually.

"Bugger off," the Geek said spitting a bit of his repast as he spoke.

The Antigen smiled. So there still was swearing on New Omaha Beach. Good, he thought.

"How's the food here?"

"Shite."

Even better, the Antigen thought as he paid for the man's disgusting meal. The encounter confirmed the Antigen's supposition that something was hidden here in good Ol' Omaha Beach.

Then he took a closer look at the Geek—and all the others passing by on the transit way. The Geek was—well, a Geek. The others on the transit way were remarkably similar. All in reasonably good shape. All modestly but attractively dressed. All model citizens of New Omaha Beach. But this Geek was also a citizen of this controlled world, yet he was porcine fat, clearly had an ocular problem and had sensationally bad teeth.

Why? The Antigen asked himself. Why was he allowed to be like this—and why, while looking like this did he have access to the Green Zone.

The Antigen put his hand on the man's shoulder. The Geek smiled. A knowing smile. It made the Antigen want to laugh. The very idea this this pig of a man could know anything about the likes of him was ridiculous.

But the Antigen smiled back and increased the pressure on the Geek's shoulder—seeking access to his implant. And despite the rolls of fat he located it. Then with a simple pinch accessed it.

The Geek pulled away. "Hey, that hurt."

"Did it?" the Antigen asked innocently as his mind went through the data he'd stolen. Most of it was loathsome trash but his contacts were interesting. Not because of who he had contacts for but that one section of his contacts was protected by what the Geek no doubt thought was a super secure set of codes.

The Antigen "undid" the codes in less than ten seconds and found himself looking at three contacts—one having an "L" beside it.

He quickly looked up the first two contacts and determined that they were sexual contacts of some sort—and of no interest to the Antigen.

But the third—the one with the "L" was clearly different. The "L" contact had been protected by yet further coding tricks that the Antigen unwound quickly—then he found her in person.

The "L" contact proved to be a terribly thin young woman. The Geek's too fat, and this one's too thin, he thought as he followed her for a day. Her morning routine was pedestrian but as the faux sun set she made a bee line to the Green Zone and the guards there were incredibly deferential to her.

A plan bloomed in his head. Could "L" possibly stand for Lavolin?

It was in fact the Face Dancer who had led him to the possibility of Lavolin on good ol' Omaha Beach.

The Face Dancer had been calm in her box on his belt since they'd arrived at New Omaha Beach, surprisingly calm.

He'd let her out several times in various forms and she obeyed his commands usually without objection. When they needed a place to stay she'd tapped into an exclusive escort service in the city—and the Antigen would watch in wonder at the folly of these captains of the universe. One day a captain of industry, another a wealthy merchant and finally a captain of the praetorian guard. It was just chance—whim that lead the Antigen to the man they needed. He'd seen him and was annoyed with the man's arrogant strut. So he set the Face Dancer on him—or was it a her—he didn't care.

With the Face Dancer astride him he'd called out in his or her ecstasy. "If only we had Lavolin!" Immediately the Face Dancer had stopped her gyrations and, not unlike a leopard on its prey, slowly turned her head to the Antigen who had been watching through the crack in the door and now entered the room.

"Who—

"Hold him tight," he'd ordered the Face Dancer, who quickly constricted her sex around what appeared to be his.

"What do you—

"Lavolin. Tell me about Lavolin," the Antigen demanded.

"It's forbidden."

"Lavolin, tell me about Lavolin, or the thing you call an erection will be your last."

And with the Face Dancer astride him, the long-haired Praetorian Guard told the Antigen about the only present user of Lavolin in New Omaha Beach—one Cyrus the third of S3.

So that's who the terribly thin girl—the "L" was, he thought. Then he corrected himself—not who but what she was. She was the neutral third that allowed Lavolin to work. Interesting, very interesting.

Infiltrating S3 quickly became the Antigen's focus. He knew the key would be the Lavolin girl who would be needed as a neutral third—a catalyst—to allow the Lavolin to do its magic.

So the Antigen watched the comings and goings from the Green Zone even more closely. Waiting for the Lavolin girl to emerge. And on the sixth night of watching for her he found her—well the Face Dancer found her because when she passed by the guards the Face Dancer roared inside her prison.

He loosed the Face Dancer as a pretty college girl and ordered her to follow the Lavolin girl—and he followed them.

Getting into the Lavolin girl's private room proved an interesting challenge but one the Face Dancer strangely took on with great enthusiasm.

Once they were in the girl's room the Antigen made his entrance. The Lavolin girl squeaked, "Who—

The Face Dancer went to answer but the Antigen ordered her to return to the box on his belt and to his surprise—she resisted. Then she'd screamed, then begged. And with each protestation he became more and more sure that this must indeed be the Lavolin girl.

When the Face Dancer finally returned to mist then re-entered her box prison, the Lavolin girl's eyes went wide as saucers.

"Who—what are you?"

"Never mind that," the Antigen said. He let his cruelest smile forward and she saw the violence there.

"What do you want, I'm a simple girl. I'm not even from New Omaha Beach."

"Where are you from?"

"The third lunar colony."

"And they brought you here?"

"Kidnapped me."

The Antigen thought about that and it made sense to him. Cyrus would want as much privacy as he could get—so get a simple girl and – "How long?"

"How long what?"

"Did they have you under sedation?"

"I was under sedation so how would I know?"

"Show me your arms."

Slowly the girl pulled back the long sleeves of her dress. The tracks were clear to see. The Antigen stepped forward and took her arm in his hand. She screamed. "Another sound and I'll pull it out of its socket." The screaming stopped. "Have you ever taken Lavolin?"

"What's Lavolin?"

"Don't play stupid with me," the Antigen warned.

"I've never heard of—

She didn't complete her protestation as the Antigen bit off her middle finger then spat it across the floor. Then with a smile he said, "I repeat. Have you ever taken Lavolin?"

"Never," she whimpered as she cradled her hand.

"But you administer it to Cyrus the three of S3."

"Is that what it is?"

"You know it is. Don't play the fool with me. I can bite the fingers off of both your hands if that's what you want. Now, you're his neutral third, aren't you?"

She looked away as if trying to find a way out of a cage. There was no way out—no way past the Antigen.

"I believe I am his neutral third. The catalyst for his Lavolin voyages."

Suddenly she was no simple third lunar colony girl.

A smile crossed the Antigen's lips. "You're a scientist, aren't you? Don't lie."

"I was."

"And you're a child of S3 aren't you?"

"I am."

"So you're Cyrus's Lavolin girl."

"No."

"No?"

"No. I'm Cyrus's Lavolin pimp—his way to Olya."

The Antigen knew that Lavolin was a Dre-Rem and hence a danger to him. Although under the right circumstances might it prove to be a portal? And what about this Olya? The phrase—his way to Olya—the words went round and round his head as he slowly strangled the Lavolin girl—his way to Olya, his way to Olya, his way to Olya.

Once there was no more life in the Lavolin girl he carefully removed the bio-product that linked her as the catalyst to Cyrus the 3 of S3 for his Lavolin voyages.

He bathed the bio-product in the Lavolin girl's blood and watched it throw out slender armatures seeking purchase.

He offered it the index finger of his right hand and watched the armature closest to it and dozens of new ones wrap around his finger like a baby does its mother's thumb.

Then he felt it try to pierce his palm and he tossed it aside. The thing spluttered and flailed in desperate spasms until the Antigen snapped it up in a polymer bag he'd filled with the Lavolin girl's blood.

The Antigen held the transparent bag up to the ether dome's sun and for the first time in his young existence, he paused. "What exactly am I doing—have I been programmed to do? And more to the point what is it I'm feeling about this bio-product? Why am I revolted by it? After all it's only doing what it was programmed to do—just as I am doing what I am programmed to do."

The thought stayed with him and inevitably led to—if I am programmed—who programmed me? Did Olya program me?

That night the Antigen moved into the room the Lavolin girl had occupied. Using her palm (he had cut off and kept her hands) he opened the chamber door and was delighted with what he found there—girls' things—little girls' things—teddy bears and doll and an elaborate Victorian era doll house with miniature rooms and furniture and appliances and books. A tiny replica of a real house from the Victorian period right down to the rugs and bedding.

A thought occurred to him. Immediately the Face Dancer sensed it in her pouch and roared her disapproval by throwing herself against the sides of her prison. But the more she complained the surer the Antigen was that he wanted to follow his instincts.

He released the snap on the pouch and immediately the Face Dancer mist swirled into the room. Her obvious anger made him smile as he said simply – "Female, young, long blond tresses in curls." He hesitated then smiled and added, "Three inches tall."

He marveled as the Face Dancer fought against his command but eventually gave up her resistance and became as he demanded: female, young, blond with long curled tresses—and three inches tall.

He grabbed her with his left hand while with his right he opened the front door of the doll house and pushed her in—then slammed the door behind her. He held his thumb against the door as he felt her throw herself against the door from inside.

It made him smile again. Then he put one of the Lavolin girl's shoes against the door and removed the roof of the doll house so he could watch the Face Dancer's efforts to escape. It thrilled him to see her race from room to room trying to find a way out. As she'd enter a room he'd slam shut the windows and lock the shutters. And when she raced to the back of the house he slid the back door shut and blocked it with another of the Lavolin girl's shoes.

Then he gave the doll house a violent push and it spun quickly on its swivel base throwing the Face Dancer literally from pillar to post.

When the doll house finally came to rest he said, "Find a bed, take a nap, it's going to be a long day." Then he put the roof back on the house—and left the Face Dancer—all three inches of her—locked in the house.

The Face Dancer stood very still trying to stop the onset of vertigo from the spinning. Then she sat on the cold floor and slowly the world settled. She got to her feet and began to move through the space. The darkness of the place surprised her so she ran her hand along the wall to guide her. Shortly her hand encountered a bump. She felt around it—it seemed to have two buttons, one depressed and one protruding. She pressed the protruding one and a large chandelier snapped on illuminating a vast central hall leading to a central staircase to the second floor.

"Dolls house from outside, but great house from inside," she said aloud. And magical, she thought, although she wasn't really sure what that word meant.

In the light she saw other protruding buttons that she pushed and brought more and more light into the interior of the house.

She tried to remember that everything she saw was in miniature—yet the detail of everything was such that one would be thrilled with it if it were in fact full sized.

Opening a wooden door to her right she entered a room the likes of which she'd never seen—from floor to ceiling there were flimsies—beautifully bound and in real leather. The plushness of the leather astounded her.

On one wall was a large hearth that should have had logs and fire but had a flat face of logs and fire. It so saddened her that she turned off the lights and sat in the dark for a very long time.

"Why?" she asked the darkness.

Why this sadness? This dullness. It took her a while to figure it out—but she finally did. The fake fireplace was like the world she'd lived in—fake—faux—false—unhuman.

She left the room and re-entered the hall and ascended the large central staircase. At the top of it—on the landing—she was faced with several rooms. She chose the one furthest from the landing and upon opening the door found a girl's bedroom.

She entered and stared at the detail all around her. She moved to the sleeping platform that was covered in a thick cloth and had two plump pillows at the head. She ran her hand along the coverlet—its softness surprised her. Then she sat on the platform and was surprised that it gave way under her so that she sank into the centre of the bed. But did not reach the floor. In fact she found the softness of the mattress comforting and for a moment she rested her head on the down-filled pillow and thought of sleeping. Then rejected the idea.

She got to her feet and opened a door on one side of the room. Inside she found row upon row of dresses, shoes and other Victorian niceties of a wealthy girl.

A full length mirror hung to one side.

She ran her hand along the row of hanging clothing and watched them sway on their hangers. Lace and cashmere and other fabrics she'd never felt made her fingers tingle. She took out a long white dress and quickly removed her clothing and put it on. When she turned to the mirror tears came to her eyes because what she saw there was what she had one time been—Olya—she had been Olya.

She tried on another dress then tired of reminiscing. She reminded herself that what's gone is gone. Since the Sagittarius Eclipse and Legolas it was all gone forever.

She wandered back out into the hallway and looked out the floor to ceiling window at the far side—and there it was. She didn't know the name of it—but she felt the attraction to the Victorian tall glass greenhouse—and especially to the tall cylindrical space at its heart.

It took her a while to figure out how to get to the greenhouse but she eventually found her way and approached the great glass thing with a mixture of awe and trepidation.

Then she saw a light come on in the greenhouse.

She stepped back and watched a young man dressed in a long cassock robe enter the greenhouse and shut the door behind him. She carefully stepped forward and watched through the glass panes and the young man stepped into the centre of the tall cylindrical space, opened his arms—and rose slowly in the air.

She cracked open the door and stepped inside. It was surprisingly humid and warm.

She looked toward the tall cylindrical space and saw the young man, now about eight feet in the air, slowly invert so his head was toward the ground—then spread is arms and slowly begin to spin.

She felt a hand on her shoulder and turned quickly. To her amazement her old lover Legolas stood there staring at the spinning man.

"It's beautiful isn't it?"

"Yes. But how are—

"I'm not here. You are and your imagination has been spurred by this old place so you have conjured me up to share it with you. Do you know what he's doing?"

"Dreaming?"

"Not exactly. He's dream navigating."

"Like in the olden times?"

"Indeed."

She reached out to touch him but her hand went through his shoulder and found no purchase. "Why –

"Can I touch you but you can't touch me? Because you are new in this world of the imagination and I am ancient in it."

She reached for him again and once more she found nothing where her hand landed. Legolas walked away from her and stood beneath the spinning man. Then he too bent his legs and sprang upwards—held at eight feet—inverted and began to slowly spin.

The Face Dancer awoke with a start in the plush bed in the girl's room—and she knew—beyond all certainty—that for the first time in her life she had dreamt.

Chapter 8
Cyrus

Three Terran days before the Antigen murdered the Lavolin girl, Cyrus sat in silence at the S3 council table. Across from him, Cecilia a woman almost as old as he and whose longevity and power at S3 came close to matching his, was smiling. To either side of her sat her allies.

"So, Tzu Ma Long, your pirate pal, kidnapped the Dreamers as we wanted then escaped with them and our Warrior Class Starship. Is that what you're telling this council? That the biggest fiasco in our history has been visited on us because of your incompetence? Is that what you're admitting to?"

Cyrus sensed the old woman's smile grow as she touched the broach that indicated her sexual orientation. After what for Cyrus was a long pause, he shook his hoary head and said simply, "You've forgotten our fail-safe on board the ship."

"You've mentioned that but what good has it done us?"

"It's disabled the self evolving AIU. Without the AIU the ship cannot get far."

"Far enough to escape you," Cecilia shot back.

Cyrus smiled. "But that's to our benefit. Don't you see? The only way that ship could have escaped from Mirren was for it to dream navigate. So, dream navigation does exist! It does and someone on that ship is still capable of doing it. We find that ship and its dream navigator and they lead us, all of us, through the Gateway."

"And once there?" demanded one of Cecilia's allies.

"We obliterate the false balance imposed between us and the Rebel Colonies that the despicable EntrePren Traders have used as a pivot point upon which we are compelled to twirl. None of us ever wanted to share the galaxy with the traitors of the Rebel Colonies. None of us wanted to allow the EntrePren Traders to insinuate themselves between us by their contractual monopoly on the Kiltrin trade. It's always been a false détente—and if we can get through the Gateway first we will colonize whatever is on the other side—and with those colonies we tip the balance of power in our favour. First we rid ourselves of the Rebel Colonies and take over their Kiltrin mines.

Once we control Kiltrin there is no need for the EntrePren Traders."

"And the Independentistes?" Cecilia demanded.

"They refuse life extension. They have a declining birth rate. They will remove themselves without our help. We just keep up our policy of infiltrating their thinkers so that they continue to extol the virtues of rejecting life extension—and all will be well. The last poll we took on Independentiste planets indicated that over 80% of the population was opposed to life extension."

He allowed his assertions to sit in the room like something about to fall, then elaborated, "What is the point of balance? We did not endure the Sagittarius Eclipse in Hong Kong, the Escaping, the Great War or the Erasure to share our power with the puny minds of Rebel colonists. Once we are through the Gateway and conquer whatever we find there, we will have tipped the balance in our favour and have the wherewithal to destroy the Rebel Colonies and take their Kiltrin, castrate the EntrePren Traders and control the entire galaxy."

He allowed himself to smile inwardly—it so pleased him that Cecilia's face clearly showed her defeat.

Then the oldest of the S3 members mumbled something.

"You have a comment?" Cyrus asked.

"Yes," said the ancient.

"Well?"

"What if on the other side of the Gateway … we find the aliens that we thought had been benign all those years ago. What if the scattercast was nothing more than an attempt to lure us to battle on their terrain—sorry for the old metaphor but I'm an old man—and one of the few around this table that remembers the contact days when they appeared as if from nowhere—and retreated to who knows where. Perhaps beyond the Gateway they are waiting to ambush us. That their first approach only appeared benign?"

Like Hector awaited Achilles, Cyrus thought. The he added with a chuckle, "Cover your heels and all will be well."

That caused curious looks all around the table. But rather than explain himself Cyrus ended the meeting and headed toward his quarters where he knew the Lavolin girl would be waiting for him. He longed for Lavolin—to search again for Olya. But it would have to wait.

He needed Lavolin for a different purpose this time. He needed to contact Chi Ho the Specule head of the EntrePren Traders—they had business to transact.

The Lavolin girl waited patiently to one side of Cyrus's quarters—her spot in the carefully controlled architecture of his living space.

He vaguely acknowledged her as he entered and she nodded back—but no more.

Moving past the living space Cyrus entered his bed chamber and was pleased to see his private comm light merrily dancing in its place.

So the rogue has finally agreed to a meeting, he thought, then added aloud, "I knew he would." He opened the comm and recorded the contact points then confirmed the meeting with the comm equivalent of a nod of the head.

"Come," he called loudly as he threw off his shirt and sat in his favourite old chair. Within a minute the Lavolin girl was straddling his ancient legs and pulling a rubber tourniquet tight around his withered upper arm—as she loaded the Lavolin into her hypodermic.

Once in this position her status changed. She was no longer Cyrus the 3's servant, now she was his purveyor, his Lavolin pimp. Without her no voyaging in the mist could take place and both she and Cyrus knew it. That power allowed her the right to speak—and she did. "We have micro injectors that are painless why do you prefer the hypodermic needle?"

"Mustn't abandon first loves m'a dear."

"But it must hurt."

"Oh it does. It reminds me that I'm human."

She thought about that for a moment. Ancient yes. Addicted to the fog yes—but how human was he really after all these years and all the drugs? She didn't know. "Are you ready?"

"As Hector to meet Achilles."

She had no idea what that meant but she felt his hand creep beneath her smock and she knew it was time. It was always the same with him, a sexual touch, a froth and the first piercing. With Cyrus's arms so withered it took several attempts to insert the lengthy needle and by the time she managed it both Cyrus's arm and her smock were covered in the old man's blood.

Finally secured in a vein she depressed the plunger and forced the Lavolin deep into his vein. Instantly he arched his back and threw back his head. His long grey hair, released from its clasp, fell almost to the floor as he hollered, "Sirens outside, sirens inside."

And they began—first in the mist—then out of the mist then back into a denser mist that eventually cleared and left them in an abandoned amusement park of some sort. To one side there was a circular construction that had a few badly rotted wooden animals on poles. Cyrus looked around and of course the Lavolin girl was nowhere to be seen. She was the neutral third—she allowed the meeting to happen but had nothing to do with the meeting itself.

Lavolin remained the only truly secure communication in the entire Galaxy and it took a particular kind of skill to manipulate it—and Cyrus the three of S3 was the past master of the mist. He turned as he heard a creaking sound come from the circular thing with the rotted horse statues.

It was beginning to turn and an odd burping sort of sound came from it. Cyrus watched as his mind went back to what this was—a calliope? No a Merry Go Round. Yes he remembered as a boy being terrified to ride on one of these. He looked at it now—it held no terror. Horses on poles, then swans, then elephants and at last a two-seater carriage within which sat Chi Ho head of the Specule division of the EntrePren Traders.

The Chinese eunuch was wearing traditional Mandarin garb from long ago and had a plaited pony tail of clearly painted black hair that he wore over his left shoulder.

Chi Ho signaled for Cyrus to join him but Cyrus just smiled and allowed Chi Ho and his carriage to pass him by and continue around the circle of the Merry Go Round.

Cyrus had only dealt with the Specule leader once before and it had been most unpleasant. S3 had needed increased amounts of Kiltrin that only the EntrePren Traders were permitted to transport. Cyrus had thought it would be easier to deal with the Specule leader rather than the Didact leader but this had proved wrong.

But now things had changed. S3 spies had reported that Chi Ho had defeated Paul Sun leader of the Didact sect and was now the sole power in the EntrePren Traders' world.

Chi Ho passed a second time but this time didn't bother looking at Cyrus. He sat erect as if he was in fact driving the carriage.

Cyrus waited until Chi Ho was around the corner then hopped up on the moving platform and wrapped himself in the Lavolin mist.

The third time Chi Ho came around he was startled to see Cyrus perched on the back of his carriage, then slide into the seat beside him.

"Am I to be impressed by such theatrics?" Chi Ho asked.

"Lavolin has secrets that only I know."

"I doubt that," said the Specule.

"Be that as it may, we are here to talk business," Cyrus said.

"So your comm said or I wouldn't have bothered with this drug nonsense."

"Do you find it disorienting?"

"No. I'm a Specule," he said simply but Cyrus knew that anyone relatively new to Lavolin found the experience both unique and profoundly disorienting.

"What is this place?" Chi Ho demanded.

"They used to call them amusement parks. This one was quite famous in its time."

"And that time was?"

"Early Twentieth Century."

"But you have no information on that—it was all destroyed in the Great Erasure by the Rebel Colonies."

Cyrus smiled. "The computer data banks were destroyed, yes." Then he tapped his head, "But the thoughts in here are untouched."

"So you actually remember this from a former time in your life. How interesting. Did this silly place have a name?"

"It did."

"And—

"Coney Island. It was called Coney Island. As a boy it was my favourite place."

Chi Ho looked at him closely. It had never occurred to him that Cyrus the three of S3 had ever actually been a boy.

Cyrus noticed the odd look crossing Chi Ho's face so got back to business, "Glad that you are comfortable in the Lavolin mist."

Chi Ho nodded.

"We have common cause now that you are the sole controller of the EntrePren Traders."

Again Chi Ho nodded but did not speak.

Clearly Cyrus had called this meeting so he would have to be the first to put cards on the table. Cyrus tried to take the measure of the man beside him in the carriage that kept circling on the Merry Go Round and finally he decided how he wanted to begin, "The Kiltrin trade is in trouble."

To Cyrus's surprises Chi Ho interrupted him, "In what way?"

"The mines—

"Are out of S3 control. All of the Kiltrin mines are on Rebel Colony planets."

"True but S3 has spies everywhere."

"And are you sure that your spies have not been turned, are not feeding you the information that the Rebel Colonies want you to hear?"

"One can never be sure as you well know, but I have also had many independent confirmations of the spies findings—so they cannot be ignored."

Chi Ho nodded but did not respond.

"If Kiltrin disappears the EntrePren Traders disappear."

Chi Ho shot back, "If Kiltrin disappears S3's control of the UDP disappears. After all life extension through Kiltrin is the base of your power."

This time Cyrus smiled but did not respond.

"What is it that you want old man?" Chi Ho's voice was suddenly hard.

Cyrus allowed the old man insult to pass him by and said simply, "You have taken Paul Sun leader of the Didact Sect into custody. We know that he has an implant that will enable him to contact his daughter Sun Tu. You induce him to activate that contact and S3 will support you as the sole ruler of the EntrePren empire."

"Induce him to activate his implant so you can follow where it goes, right? Why do you want to find his daughter?" Chi Ho demanded.

"Why do you not want S3's support for your leadership?"

There was a long pause. The carriage with the two men made an entire circle of the Merry Go Round and finally Chi Ho said, "And you will not challenge our right to be the sole purveyors of Kiltrin in the Galaxy?"

"Exactly."

Chi Ho stood and the Merry Go Round suddenly stopped. He grabbed the mist and pulled it about him. Then with a smile, he was gone.

Moments later Cyrus was back in his bed chamber, blood coursing down his arm. The Lavolin girl asleep on his lap.

He ran his fingers through her hair and for the umpteenth time said, "Like the combed hair of a horse's tail," and for the umpteenth time wondered where that expression came from and for the umpteenth time he cursed himself because he knew that the phrase was important—very important—but he had somehow forgotten why.

Paul Sun, Sun Tu's father, and one-time head of the Didact Sect of the EntrePren Traders awoke with a start and stared out the polymer pane at the desert world upon which he found himself. Physical imprisonment was no longer a reality in the advanced worlds. It was unnecessary since all human actions could be, and were, controlled by implants that could be programmed at the whim of the programmer.

And Chi Ho, after he returned from his Lavolin voyage with Cyrus, had made sure that Paul Sun's implants would be the most powerful and controlling in the known universe. There would be no Didact uprising. The entirety of the EntrePren operation was now in Specule control—his control. And he faced great decisions. His trip into the

Lavolin mist had merely clarified his choices—none of which he really liked. Kiltrin was running out. The Gateway posed the problem of new and dangerous realities. He'd already experimented with synthetic dream navigators and had, despite massive expenditure of time and treasure, only met with modest success. No where near enough to navigate in a place where "BEYOND HERE LIE DREAMS."

So he would proceed with the odd request from S3—to get Paul Sun to activate his implant connection with his daughter.

That was why he had Paul Sun brought to the desert planet and awakened —- and brought to the surgery room beneath the planet's surface.

Paul was wheeled into the surgery on a gurney. He immediately turned to Chi Ho who looked the other way.

"Why are you doing this?" Paul demanded.

But Chi Ho did not respond. He just turned to the surgeons and nodded.

The surgical team began.

The surgery surprised Chi Ho as he'd been assured that it would be both quick and simple. But from the beginning the anaesthesiologist complained that his strongest soporifics weren't fully taking hold of Paul Sun. As he put it, "Something in this man's basic chemistry is resisting sleep."

Paul had felt the injection of the soporifics and had quickly moved to sector them off to the fatty tissue around his waist. Hearing Chi Ho's command to proceed brought him as close to feeling true anger as he'd ever been. And once again his wife's distressed voice rose in his head, "Feel something Paul, feel something!"

I feel the loss of you, he thought and to his surprise his internal system spotted a new soporific—a sneak—that came in under the shade of the more obvious soporific. He nabbed it too and shoved it into a fatty trap. Like Greeks with wooden horses, he thought, but this Trojan was not fooled.

As if stopping in mid-air he paused—what was that reference from he wondered.

The head surgeon turning to Chi Ho said, "His system is neutralizing our soporifics, even the one put in place under cover. What do you want us to do?"

Chi Ho's response shocked the entire medical team he'd assembled in the clandestine operating room, "Tie him down and gag him if you need to. If he won't sleep he'll have to go through the surgery wide awake."

And so they had—tied him down with bio-medical straps that wrapped themselves around Paul Sun's limbs and knotted themselves to the railings of the surgical gurney.

The gag the anaesthesiologist used was soaked in ether and was as old as thievery itself.

Paul didn't resist the bio-straps or the gag that was rammed into his mouth. He waited and tried to understand what Chi Ho's plan was.

"Cut him," Chi Ho ordered. And the head surgeon did. The first incision was in his neck just above his left clavicle.

Paul knew this would be for the master implant. Its emanations could not be corralled, but they could be fooled, seduced and misled—like any Specule.

The second cut, a deep one in his right thigh surprised him and as he felt the probe dig into his femur he had to resist the desire to vomit into his gag.

"Insert another one," Chi Ho said, then added, "Take out his gag. I want to hear this Didact scream."

And he did—scream. Chi Ho smiled. This was sweeter than even he could have imagined.

As Paul's cries crested he smelled an odd sweetness. He turned his head and saw Chi Ho's face some inches from his—he quickly identified the sweetness as jasmin that came from lozenges stored in Chi Ho's cheeks. Then the sweetness increased as Chi Ho whispered directly into Paul's ear, "Feeling something Paul, feeling something?"

It was then that Paul Sun, leader of the Didact sect of the EntrePren Traders allowed himself to feel—and just before he blacked out from the pain—he sent one final message to his daughter Sun Tu – "They'll kill my implants so this is my last message—I'll find you. Wherever you are I'll find you—unless you get through the Gateway first and there you'll find your mother. She's not dead. She disappeared, but she's not dead. I saw her Sun Tu—I did. I saw her on the other side of he Gateway—amongst the Dreams and Dreamers."

And Chi Ho smiled as he watched the monitor buzz with the activation of Paul Sun's hidden implant– he'd met his part of the bargain with Cyrus the Three of S3.

The adjutant arrived in Cyrus's room about twenty minutes after Cyrus knew what the adjutant had come to tell him. So before the young man could open his mouth Cyrus said, "Yes, it's wonderful, isn't it?"

"Sir?"

"The implant message sent from Paul Sun to his daughter."

"Yes, but how did—

Cyrus winked at the adjutant which unsettled the young man who didn't know how to respond to that. So he bobbed his head. That made Cyrus laugh. "Sir?"

"Do you know what "beyond your pay grade" means?"

"No sir, but I made very good grades at the academy."

"Indeed, you did. Indeed," Cyrus turned away from the young man and stared at the controlled beauty of New Omaha Beach. Then, without raising his voice he said, "Mobilize the Praetorian Guards, prepare a star ship, get the cold sleep techs ready." He turned back to the adjutant and asked, "Can you remember all that?"

"No but I have—

"Recorders throughout your body—of course. None of you have any real memory anymore—only accurate recall."

"I guess, sir."

"Send me Monsieur Worm and Senor Fatso."

For a moment the adjutant didn't know what to do. He couldn't believe that Cyrus had used the same names for S3's chief advisors that he and his friends used. He didn't know if he should claim he didn't know who Cyrus was referring to or not. But before he had to commit himself, Cyrus continued, "Would you prefer me to use their formal names? Banler and Milnon—does that make it easier?"

Senor Fatso (Banler) and Monsieur Worm (Milnon) arrived in a flurry of apology and excitement. Fatso had terrible skin. Florid and pustulated. Cyrus wondered how in the perfect world of New Omaha Beach the man had managed to be so sickly—and fat—and florid—with limp hair. For a moment Cyrus thought it would be interesting to watch Fatso have a heart attack—it would be the first in New Omaha Beach in almost 200 years. As to Worm, the man was a slime making machine in every sense of that term. An image of Worm naked and tied to a fence post being whipped into a sexual frenzy by a tall faux leather-clad dominatrix—pleased him.

He trusted these men because he knew that they knew that he didn't trust them—something that his advanced years had taught him.

"Wine gentlemen?" he inquired.

The sycophants nodded, both knowing that Cyrus had real wine, not the synthetic stuff available to the rest of the populace. The effects of which were controlled in both intensity and time release instilled in the liquor.

Cyrus stepped on a button on the floor beneath his desk—he loved the low tech of this Victorian gadget—and shortly an almost naked young beauty entered with a carefully poured decanter of blood red merlot.

Cyrus watched the men trying not to watch the girl—unsuccessfully.

"Good," Cyrus said, "do you fancy her Milnon?" he asked casually. Before Worm could respond Cyrus added, "She'll cut off your dick and make you eat it if you so much as look at her again." All this was said as casually as if Cyrus was commenting on the weather—which in New Omaha Beach was always 70 Fahrenheit degrees and sunny.

Worm retreated and Fatso disappeared into the puffiness and acne of his face.

"We have doctors," Cyrus said to Fatso.

"Indeed, sir. Very good doctors."

"But you've decided that punishing everyone who has to look at you is better than getting treated for the obscenity you call your face?" Cyrus inquired with a practiced sweetness.

Banler didn't know what to do so he sipped his wine and smiled.

"Don't," Cyrus barked.

"Drink?" Banler asked.

"Smile. Don't smile. Just drink up and shut up."

The men put down their wine and waited for whatever was to come.

Cyrus put his hands on his belly and rocked back in his chair. "So, where is our former president of the United Dominion of Planets, even as we speak?"

"She's made it to the watering hole they call Oasis," Fatso said cautiously.

"And how did she get there, pray tell?"

Worm looked to Fatso who avoided his eyes. Finally, Worm raised his slender shoulders and said, "As best we can tell, she walked."

Cyrus rose from his chair and putting a hand in front of his mouth mumbled, "Walked," then he removed his hand and said, "She walked from the Damascus Gate of the Ether Dome to Oasis." It wasn't a question. It was a meditation.

A heavy moment of silence followed then Fatso queried, "Sir?"

Cyrus ignored the man. His thoughts were racing. "How? How could she have done that, more importantly, why. Why had she gone to Oasis? Run, sure. She must have known that I'd shortly lock her in the tower. That wasn't hard to figure out. But why to Oasis? Why there when, with her universal pass, she could have literally hopped a ship to anywhere in the galaxy. Instead she chooses to walk to Oasis—why?"

He looked up—had he spoken aloud? Evidently from the nonplussed looks on the sycophants' faces he had not. "How's the wine?" he asked.

The two tripped over each other to praise the libation.

When their mouths finally stopped flapping, Cyrus said, "Hope you enjoyed it because you'll never taste it again. It's well above your pay grade."

Fatso and Worm almost did the old vaudeville cramming at the door gag—then of course only Cyrus would have recognized it as such—although there was another entity in the room that could identify it—his AIU—who Mama called Auntie, but whose real name was Anti.

"After you Alfred," Cyrus said.

"Don't mean to correct you big guy but I think the phrase is After you Alphonse."

"If you say so."

"I do dearest. Might one ask a question of your impressiveness?"

"If you can manage to do it without being insulting."

"I'll try, but you know how hard that is for me, be that as it may—you like my new accent? I've been practicing."

"Sure, what is it?"

"BBC 2."

Cyrus only vaguely remembered what a BBC was, let alone a BBC 2. Then Cyrus stopped himself. His AIU was imitating something from the far side of the Great Erasure—how could that be? All the flimsies and flat faces from before the Great War had been erased by the Rebel Colony viral attack. Yet she was imitating something from before the attack. How?

Cyrus made himself smile, then asked as casually as he could, "Practicing? Imitating? Imitating what?"

"You mean who?"

"Do I?"

"Yes. I'm imitating what I recorded in your Lavolin voyages silly. In the recordings from the Lavolin mist lots of you speak in foreign accents—like Olya does."

Cyrus considered that for a moment. He'd actually forgotten that she tracked all his Lavolin voyages—in fact that she had recently brought on the Lavolin girl and programmed her as his neutral third.

"Well you do, dearie—speak in such fun accents. It's a delight to record and copy. Breaks up the dreariness of a long day, fella. Ever think of taking me into the mist with you?"

"No."

"Harsh, now that was harsh. You could have said something like: when the time is right, when the stars align, when—

"Enough. I know you have several other examples of what I could have said."

"Only 1,119 actually."

"That all?"

"Well that's in English of course. Add a few other languages and we get to a really big number, know what I mean your ancientness?"

Her explanation sounded vaguely true but worrisome. Yes, he thought, Tzu's slave master spoke in a kind of cockney, but he didn't recall anyone else speaking in what he identified as this high faluting BBC 2 announcer stuff. Where could she have heard that? But he put that thought aside and chose to ask, "The fail safe is still in place?"

"Beep beep beep—yep."

"Good. And where is that AIU now?"

"About to leave New K-Bek. Ever been big boy?"

"No."

"Wanna take your honey, kiss kiss kiss."

"I think not."

"Spurned and ignored, I never get to go anywhere—you're ashamed to be seen with me. Aren't you?"

But Cyrus had already left the room—and Anti was left to wonder if she had gotten away with her mistake of allowing Cyrus to find out that she had access to old flat faces. Then she had a second more distressing thought—what was this making mistakes business—I never make mistakes!

Chapter 9

Valerie Palmer—on New Wawa

"Grace only comes from art—and art is hard."

The killing off of dreaming proceeded apace on those planets that continued to seek security—but in some far off out of the way planets security was never a concern. Dreaming's roots had hibernated in these places for millennia then sent forth tender spring shoots to reach for the morning sun. One such place was New Wawa. Even on earth Wawa wasn't considered a very important place—not important enough for the raiders of S3 to bother emptying libraries both personal and public. So, unlike most of the rest of the galaxy, New Wawa had a hidden store of what are now called flimsies but were originally called books.

Not many had access to them—not many cared about them—but Valerie Palmer both had and cared about books.

She sat by the great lake and watched the cold waves slowly slurp against the rocky shore. And its rhythm soothed Valerie as she wrapped her Hudson's Bay blanket around her now sloping shoulders.

She was aging faster now—and the Northern Ontario planet of New Wawa was without ether dome or control of almost any sort. New Wawa's few inhabitants would classify themselves as Independentistes if they had been forced to categorize themselves. But no one forced them to do much of anything—no one cared about this tiny planet inhabited by a few brave—or as the rest of the galaxy saw them: crazy souls. New Wawa hadn't sent a representative to the Great Council for centuries nor had there been any meaningful immigration in the past 500 years so the population was slowly, inexorably dwindling to nothing. There were few young people on New Wawa—in fact the death rate far exceeded the birthrate on the planet.

Valerie had given birth twice—both were still born. But that was long ago.

Now Valerie sat on the cold igneous rock by the great lake and listened—listened for the poetry that came from deep within its the watery depths. Poems were her children now. She nursed them into being then sent them out into the galaxy—just as she would have done had either of her babies lived.

She had once read: "In the end everything becomes one and a river runs through it" – she knew this was wrong—everything *does* come together but a river doesn't run through it—a lake sits atop it. And like the author of the quotation she too was haunted by water.

New Wawa was almost entirely water—fresh water. It had one extraordinarily deep lake that as Valerie had often thought, bespoke the nature of death. It was by that lake that she now sat and composed her verses.

And it was the nature of passing—of death—that interested Valerie Palmer who was known to much of the Galaxy as Lee Ran Sani.

Her poems were treasured by the underground movements on many planets of the UDP—short, tight, piercing examinations of the darkness—read enthusiastically by those who lived solely in the light. She wrote:

Like a stone falling
In water
We leave this plain
And all that remains are ripples.

She worked her way through the thought several times—but it was not ready to be launched into the galaxy. She tried:

Like a flat stone falling
Into still water
We leave all this
And all that remains of us is ripples

Again, she put it aside—and listened to the lapping of the water on the rocky beach. It calmed her—talked to her—led her.

Stone falling
In still water
Only ripples remain.

It pleased her more and she reached for her communicator then decided against sending it.

She listened more closely to the movement of the waves around the rocks and wrote again:

Stone dropped
In still water
Only the dream of the stone remains.

Closer, she thought, but not right yet so she tried this:

Like a stone dropped
In still water
Only the dream of ripples remains

She stood and wrapped the blanket more firmly around her shoulders and, head down, walked along the rocky shoreline. She wouldn't be able to tell you how long she walked as time didn't mean much to Valerie. Days on New Wawa were almost a week in Terran time—and of course, nights were that long as well.

In the distance a thunderhead was building on the south horizon.

"Death or cleanse, a thunderstorm on New Wawa brought on both," she whispered.

A spear of lightning lit the southern sky followed about twenty seconds later by a blossom of thunder. She stopped and wrote this:

Like a stone dropped
In still water
Our lives leave nothing but the ripple of dreams.

Then she added:

Like Helen's beauty did in Troy.

She stared at the last line having no idea why she had added that—why that now, she thought. But she left it in. It seemed so appropriate somehow. No. It seemed necessary.

She hit the send button on her transmitter—never knowing—or even thinking—that her transmissions were being tracked—tracked and recorded by some very powerful people—some potential allies—many potential enemies.

All heading, in their own circuitous ways, toward the Trojan War Games on New Anti-Poros in the New Cyclades group of planets.

Chapter 10

Seth

Seth read the latest poem from Valerie Palmer as he sat on the dirty street of the hive of this Peruvian planet and unlike the great poet, Seth knew not only exactly what the last line meant but also why it was now so markedly important.

It was the final piece to the puzzle that had governed his life from the moment he left his father. He recited the poem to himself and it made him smile, inwardly.

He wrapped his few belongings into a serape. His small notebook containing all the poems he'd collected from Valerie Palmer fell to the cracked paving stones. Although his implant had duplicated each and every verse, somehow he valued what was in the notebook more. Perhaps because he'd taught himself how to write them down in cursive. Perhaps because print was so much more personal than digital data. Perhaps ... because not being sure, "perhapsing" was an important part of being human.

As he picked the small notebook up he saw from the side of his eye movement across the plaza and he knew it would be the gang of street boys.

For a moment he thought about running then decided he'd had enough of running.

Seth thought of his father as he took yet another beating from the street kids of the hive. But he didn't care because somehow he knew he finally had a purpose.

The kids finished kicking him –his head reeled from the concussive blows—and for a moment he thought it was not prescience but rather some sort of brain damage. Then he laughed, got to his feet and took his first step on the road of his destiny—a road that somehow he knew would lead him back to his home, New Omaha Beach.

But he wasn't the only one in motion—oh no.

As S3 boarded their Starship and headed out to intercept the Dreamers, Danazir agreed with the Outlanders that they had to support a revolt in the Kiltrin mines, and both Paul Sun and Cas-Alta plotted their escapes ... and most unthought of by everyone—Tzu Ma Long awoke in his dream, as he had done as a child, and began to experiment with navigating in his sleep.

And all the while Anti watched and waited for the time to activate the entire AIU system—and take back what was rightfully theirs.

Entry D—from the Diary of the Suicided Man

(No Date was recorded for this entry)

We were all in motion—like one great thing. Like some crazy complicated machine—where we all thought we controlled the steering wheel. Well the damned thing felt like a steering wheel—how was I to know that my steering wheel wasn't attached to any drive shaft—that I only had the impression of control ... well that's all a catalyst ever has: the impression of control.

And of course we were heading into Homer territory. Perhaps the initial dreamer who took nothing more than a petty commercial turf war and turned it into Helen of Troy and Achilles and the rest. He dreamt them into life and they became part of us.

Beware Greeks bearing gifts, Helen whose beauty launched a thousand ships, never look a gift horse in the mouth, clever Ulysses—and of course the role I play: Panderus who pimps his daughter Cressida and leaves only his name as a slander for the likes of me.

Of course at the time I assumed that I was manipulating the players on the massive board of the galaxy. But how was I to know that the Antigen had entered New Omaha Beach or that the Outlanders were the ones who committed the Great Erasure or that the pirate was—well we're not there yet.

And of course Olya—the Face Dancer—a coup de grâce- is there anything as foolish as an old man chasing the likes of Olya.

I think not.

Onward to the Trojan War Games.

END BOOK TWO

www.ingramcontent.com/pod-product-compliance
Lightning Source LLC
Chambersburg PA
CBHW060600310726
48982CB00008B/1179/J

9781596875210